For the kind hearted

Special thanks to:

Ben and Iola Gbadamosi, Anne Adaba,
Osaretin Oswlad Guobadia, Kola Tubosun,
Geoff Ryman, Dick Cartmel, Zoë Apostolides,
Lisa Moylett, Sarah Williams, and Sofia Alexandrache.

Chapter 1

The Strange Letter

I will not finish telling this story.

I returned to my desk and found a red envelope on my laptop keyboard. My name was handwritten on it in blue ink in a beautiful scroll that must have taken time to do: Master Osaretin Osagiemwenagbon. The last time I was addressed as master was in primary school. There was no stamp and no return address, and the envelope wasn't sealed. I imagined that one of my colleagues in the open plan office had waited for me to leave before placing the envelope there. I suspected it was Rachel, and I suspected she was looking at me. I tried to hide my smile as I opened it.

I pulled out a folded piece of light purple paper. It smelt of… I sniffed it. Lavender. I couldn't hide my smile. She was probably watching. I unfolded the paper. The same beautiful writing swirled across the page.

Dear son of my late friend,

I will pay you a visit shortly, the purpose of which is to instruct you in the magic that your father was known and famous for.

Our meeting has been set for tomorrow, provided that

it does not rain on you, you do not touch a frog, and you do not know a woman before then. You must also abstain from putting your hand inside the finger – I do hope you never ever do this.

Yours magically, Brother Moses,

Most magnificent magician of the second to the highest level of all magicians.

I read it over. Two things were clear. Firstly, it was a joke, and secondly, Rachel wasn't responsible. She knew better than to make a joke that involved my late father. I read the message one last time. It could have been funny if they hadn't mentioned him. Holding the letter, I looked around. No one was watching me. No one looked as though they were suspiciously 'not-watching' me.

I put the purple paper back in its envelope, fetched my laptop bag from under the desk and slid the envelope into one of its inner compartments. By the time I was done rolling up my power cable I'd forgotten all about it.

As always, I did not drive straight from Ikoyi to Ajah. At that time, when the majority of the Lagos island workforce finished for the day, it would have taken me at least two to three hours to get home. That's two to three hours of burning precious petrol in crawling traffic. Two to three hours of looking about, afraid that at any moment armed robbers on motorbikes would smash my window, take my phone, my wallet, my money, and maybe even shoot me, just because. Better to spend longer on the island and then do a thirty-minute high-speed drive home.

I went to the Fly Bar in Victoria Island. Hassan and Bowale were already on their second bottles of Star when I got there. As Laide, the fourth member of our group, had not yet arrived, Hassan and Bowale were talking about what they would like to do with Laide's new girlfriend. I didn't have a girlfriend so I never worried over what they talked about when I wasn't there.

The thin waitress with thick framed glasses that made her look like a rocket scientist moonlighting in a beer parlour brought my half-finished bottle of red wine from the day before. I held up the glass to inspect it. I suspect that sometimes they don't bother to wash used cups. I imagined they just wiped them dry with a dirty cloth. As I looked into the glass, I saw a face looking at me. I looked up. The most beautiful, chocolate-skin, long-haired, sweetly perfumed woman asked if she could join us, and before any one of us could respond, she sat opposite me in the chair that was meant for Laide.

She was beautiful. So, so beautiful. I would never have been able to say hi to her. None of us would have been able to. She had an open bottle of wine in one hand, the same bottle as mine, and a full glass in the other. I hadn't noticed her when I walked into the Fly Bar and I'd never seen her there before. There were many empty tables, what was she doing asking to sit with us? Us. Could she be a prostitute? If she was, she was a well-dressed one. She was in a one-piece body-hugging beige dress that stopped a few inches above her knees - her legs were amazing. She

13

had a beige leather bag and beige suede shoes. She looked like a banker. I'd heard of girls who preyed on the island's big boys. We weren't island big boys. Also, if she was a prostitute, Madam Kike would have spotted her and asked her to come outside for a talk. Madam Kike never missed an opportunity to let it be known that she did not want her bar to become that kind of place. I looked around for the no-nonsense, heavily made-up owner. I desperately hoped she wasn't a prostitute. But why had she asked to sit with us?

'Do you always have wine?' she asked me.

Bowale and Hassan were staring and holding their glasses as if for support. I could see why. She was shapely, which Bowale liked, and she was dark-skinned, really, really dark-skinned, which Hassan liked. I liked everything about her. Everything. I'd not felt like that in a long time. It was like primary school falling-in-love. My heart was so fast that I felt it pounding up into my throat. She was out of my league, and I knew I would stay awake all through the night thinking of her. It was as if she'd cast a spell on me.

I meant to answer but I just stared, so she continued, 'I asked the woman at the bar for a good bottle of red. She recommended this one. I asked how she knew it was good. She said because the customer who knows wine always asks for it. Are you that customer?'

I think I nodded.

She stretched her hand to me across the table.

14

'Hi. I'm Adesua.'

She was Edo too!

I shook her hand and managed to say my name, 'Osaretin.'

'Edo,' she said. Her face brightened. I blushed under my black skin. Bowale introduced himself: 'Bowale Mogaji. CEO, Blue Star Investments.'

Nobody asked what he did for a living. She shook his hand.

Hassan was next. 'Hassan Lawal. Medical doctor.'

He too! She shook hands with him and turned her attention back to me. 'And you?' she said.

'Me? I'm in IT.'

'Yeah? Me too. I'm an IT project manager. What about you?'

I had never been so ashamed to say what I do. 'I am a programmer,' I said in a low voice while looking away, and I hoped she didn't hear it. From the corner of my eye I searched her face for disappointment. Before she could say anything else Bowale started talking to her about her investment portfolio, the commodities market, diversification, and meeting up to discuss her options. His big talk had never been so well-timed.

I downed the last of my wine. She had been listening to Bowale who was now talking about the time he went to France to collect a client's private jet that he'd helped finance. She barely turned her face away from him as she poured me a full glass from her bottle. She had been paying attention to me. In fact, I hadn't even placed the empty glass back on the table before she lifted her bottle to top me up.

Hassan tried to start a discussion about collecting contemporary art by Nigerian artists. When he tried to remember the name of the female painter who was 'hot right now' and whose two early paintings he'd bought, Bowale started talking about the small private airports between France and Lagos where the plane had to stop to refuel because it was a mid-range jet. I'd heard the story before. He left out the part where it was his former boss who helped arranged the purchase of the jet for a former governor who had since been jailed for corruption. Boys' code meant that Hassan and I let it slide.

'That sounds so exciting,' Adesua said when Bowale finally finished the story at touchdown in the private wing of Murtala Muhammad Airport.

'Yeah, you could say so. But such things are not un-common, considering my clientele.'

I could have picked up my empty wine bottle and smashed it over his balding head.

'What about you, anything exciting happen to you lately?' Adesua asked me. I could just imagine how Bowale and Hassan must have felt. They were hard at work trying to outdo each other with their embellished sales pitches yet she kept returning to me. Me. I was on the verge of admitting the lacklustre disappointment my life had turned out to be when I remembered the red envelope. As luck would have it, my laptop case was under the table. I always took it out of the car. Although both the car and the laptop belonged to the bank and were covered by insurance, when it came to the laptop the bank would, by policy, cover its loss by deducting the purchase price from my salary. A whole month's salary.

'Someone left a strange letter on my table today,' I said. I had the floor at strange letter. I took a sip of the wine which she had poured for me. They all waited to hear about my letter. 'It was in a red envelope. It said I would be visited tomorrow to be taught magic. It was signed by a Brother Moses, most magnificent magician of the second to the highest level of all magicians.'

It was a good story. I knew it. It didn't have private jets or private airstrips, but it had magic. Magic trumps jets. And paintings.

'Bullshit,' Bowale said after a pause.

I'd been anticipating that. I reached for my laptop bag under the table. I was about to play my ace. I relished their rapt silence as I opened the bag, retrieved the envelope, placed it down on a dry spot on the table, and returned the laptop bag to the ground. I'd already won but I wanted to enjoy every moment of my victory. I carefully opened the envelope as if I was handling ancient papyrus. Pinching the purple letter by the edge, I slowly pulled it out. I unfolded it. It was blank. I turned the paper round but there was nothing written on the other side either. Panic. I checked in the envelope again. I pushed its edges together to open it up wide. I turned it upside down to shake out the real letter. The envelope was empty.

Bowale took the paper from me. I saw the smirk on his face. I searched in my laptop case. There had to be an explanation.

'You started drinking at work?' Bowale said.

I thought Hassan's laughter was louder than it should have been.

Adesua stood up and picked her handbag off the table. At that moment I felt like crying.

'What's your number?' she asked.

She was looking at me when she said it. She was talking to me. She wanted my number – even after I'd managed to look stupid. I started reciting my number then I stopped after the first three digits and waited for her to get her phone out. She didn't. Instead, she said, 'Go on.' I felt stupid reading out my number to someone who wasn't storing it into her phone.

'Hope to see you guys again,' she said, and she left.

You guys, she said. You guys. Not me, Osaretin, but Bowale and Hassan and maybe me as well. If only I'd not talked about that stupid letter.

We all watched as she walked out. She passed Laide walking in through the entrance. Bowale had handed the paper to Hassan who was also holding it up to the light to confirm that it lacked the words I'd claimed had covered it. Bowale made a remark, at my expense, which they were both laughing at. It was mockery.

I went over every word of the stupid letter in my mind. It was a practical joke and it would have bought me more time with Adesua, but now I blamed whoever was behind it for my gaffe, not that they knew I would have tried to use it to impress a woman, and I no longer saw the funny side of it. It said the meeting to teach me magic would go ahead tomorrow if it did not rain on me. It was December. It had not rained for weeks and it wouldn't rain for months. They didn't even bother with that little detail. I felt stupid for bringing up the letter and I felt confused that it was now blank. But mostly I felt stupid.

Laide sat down where Adesua had sat. His face, his arms, his clothes, all were soaking wet.

'What happened to you?' Bowale asked.

Laide drew the back of his hand across his wet forehead.

'It's raining like hell in Ikoyi,' he said.

Chapter 2

Ultraviolet and Biography

On my tenth birthday my father finally showed me how he made the money disappear. It was my birthday present. He made me promise not to show anyone how it was done. I was terrible at it. Every time I tried to do the trick, the kids at school always knew I'd hidden the note in my other palm. Dad could also make money appear in a handkerchief, and throw an egg up and catch it in his palm but when he opened his fingers the egg wasn't there. He didn't teach me how to do those tricks. He was not a magician-magician. He was a doctor. He only did his tricks for my cousins and me when we were little. He died in a car crash in London just after I turned thirteen. He was buried there. I have never been to London so I have never visited his grave.

The stupid letter had reminded me of my dad.

When I turned twenty-eight, my mum said that I was becoming more and more like him. Her face, when she said it, didn't show if she thought it was a good thing or a bad thing. She never remarried, there had never been a boyfriend, and she had never even been on a date since my dad died. As far as I knew, I was the only man in her life.

She spoke little about dad after the accident, and when she did it was through necessity rather than from reflection. She would say, for instance, 'Your aunty is coming to visit you today.' And when I asked 'Which aunty?' she would say, 'Your father's brother's wife.' Even as a child I found it strange that none of my dad's brothers or sisters or any blood relatives ever came to see us. To see me. It was always a husband or a wife, or a friend of a brother or a friend of a sister. This oddity was nothing, however, compared to mum's failure to mourn. I have tried but I cannot remember seeing her cry over dad's death in faraway London. I cried. I remember her watching me cry. She picked me from school in dad's car. We stopped at Leventis where she bought me an ice cream. Vanilla, I remember. I noticed she was very quiet but licking my ice cream before it melted in the afternoon heat kept me occupied. A lot of people were in our house when we got home. A lot of them had been crying. The women stretched their hands out to me. Mum led me through them into her and dad's room, sat me on his chair and sat on the bed to face me and calmly said, 'Daddy had an accident in London last week. He died this morning.' After that she just watched me until I started crying.

There was a strange look of curiosity on her face as she watched me. As if she was searching for something on my face. Her detached, clinical inspection of my wailing haunted me for years after.

As I grew older I thought of him less, and her strange

behaviour following his death worried me less. For bringing it all back I was doubly angry at whoever left that letter on my desk. It was a prank, no doubt, and a gang of conspirators in the office were going to pay for it. The disappearing ink was genius, I admit. The unexpected December rain was a lucky coincidence. But referring to my late dad was just wrong.

The next day at work I nodded my way through my early morning meeting while planning my revenge. There had to be an Act Two to the prank. I had to find a way to turn it round on them. Immediately after the meeting I put the light purple paper into the middle of a notebook and went down to the banking hall. Normally, non-banking members of staff such as IT personnel are not allowed behind the counters in the banking hall, but I still had the code to get through the door, so no one challenged me.

I'd taken a new cashier through the banking system a week ago. I went to her cubicle. She'd flirted with me the week before. I remember being surprised when she stood from her chair and she was a lot taller than me. In fact, she was much, much taller than most of the men she worked with.

The cashier smiled and spread her hands for a hug when she saw me coming. I asked if I could quickly check something. I put the paper under the ultraviolet light used to check suspicious currency notes. I remembered from primary school that invisible ink could be seen under UV lights. I didn't see anything on either side of the paper. It occurred to me that there's probably a difference between disappearing ink and invisible ink. I'd hoped that defeating the pranksters in this little way would mark the start of my total victory over them.

Dismayed, I thanked the very tall girl and began to leave when my phone started vibrating. Thank God it was on silent, as workers are not allowed to have their phones on them behind the counter. I hurried out into the banking hall to take the call. The number was withheld. I answered it all the same. A female voice said, 'Is that you?'

I looked around for who it was that could see me, even as I tried to place the voice. 'Who is this?' I said.

'It's me, Adesua.'

She was standing by the door, holding her phone to her ear with one hand and waving with the other. She was beautiful. Even more beautiful than yesterday evening. I hoped she couldn't notice my heart pounding as I stood in front of her and held out my hand for a handshake.

'What are you doing here?' I said, trying to sound cool.

She ignored my hand and went in for a full-on hug instead. It felt great. Her hair smelt luxuriously sweet. Her voice, when she said 'good morning' into my ear, sounded like the most beautiful thing I'd ever heard.

'What are you doing here?' she threw my question back at me.

'I work here.'

'I thought you were in IT.'

'Yeah. I'm in the IT department. What about you,

what are you doing here?'

'Look at you, head office IT guru.' She squeezed my shoulder. 'I came to cash a cheque. I was just leaving when I saw you. Is that the letter?'

Adesua took the purple paper from me and held it up to inspect it.

'You still don't know who sent it?' she asked.

'No, but I know it's one of my colleagues. It's a practical joke. I knew it was a joke, I just didn't know they used disappearing ink.'

'I know you knew it was a joke.'

I started over-analysing. Why did she say she knew I knew it was a joke? Why did I even say it myself? I shouldn't have said it. Saying it suggested that I didn't know it was a joke. Was she being patronising by saying she knew I knew? No, that's not the word. She was being kind. Polite. I was pathetic. She probably actually meant, we both know you thought the letter was something other than a prank, but let's just say you knew it was a prank.

'So, who is Brother Moses?' she said.

'Who?'

'The person who is meant to teach you magic. You said you know it's a prank. Who is Brother Moses? Who wrote the letter?'

'Oh. I haven't found out.'

'So they don't know that you know?'

'I guess not. They think I chopped.' Was she playing along or was I playing along?

25

'So the prank is still on?'

'I guess you could say so.'

'That's cool. I want to know how it ends.'

She seemed genuinely and innocently interested.

'What time do you do lunch?' she said.

'Around one.'

'One? Want to meet for lunch? Maybe you would have met Brother Moses by then.'

'One is fine. Where?'

'Let's see. You work here, I work in Dolphin Estate. The Ikoyi Club is halfway.'

I wasn't a member of the Ikoyi Club. Of course, a girl like her would be a member. Her parents were probably members, as were the people she hung out with, no doubt.

Did she see the apprehension creeping into my soul?

She said, 'Or we could have a coffee now, seeing as I'm here. Just next door. Can you take a break now?'

I couldn't.

'Yes,' I said.

We walked together to the coffee shop next to the bank and both ordered cappuccinos. She pointed out how it was the second thing we had in common. Red wine, and now coffee. Then she corrected herself. We had three things in common. We were also both Edo.

I remember a day in secondary school when a new girl whose family had migrated from Fiji joined our school. Fiona. She was awesomely beautiful, as teenage girls are awesomely beautiful to teenage boys. The school didn't yet have a desk for her so Mrs Oyawoye asked if she could share mine. Our chairs were side by side behind my desk. We both had one leg under the desk and one leg outside. To achieve this sharing of space, she had to pull her skirt even higher up her thighs. Our shoulders, our arms, and our legs touched. Mrs Oyawoye pointed her ruler at me and asked me to answer the question on something that must have had to do with the geography lesson – I wasn't listening. I didn't know what the question was, so needless to say I didn't know the answer, but I had a stronger reason not to stand up.

It was geography class all over again as I had coffee with Adesua that day. I could not remember the last time I had felt that way. I was embarrassed, in love, and afraid, all at the same time.

She was telling me about her job in PR in England before she moved back to Nigeria.

'I've just been talking and talking,' she said. She dropped her hand from under her chin and rested her fingers on my hand on the table. I felt a tingle flow from her fingers, through my skin to the warm mug I was holding, and on to the other hand.

'Tell me if I'm talking too much,' she said.

I shook my head. To attempt to talk would have been to expose my current situation.

'Babes.' She drew her fingers over my arm as she lifted her hand.

'Can we see each other tonight? After work?'

'Yeah.'

I had to be cool. I had to be cool.

'Great. I'll call you at six.'

I nodded. I was afraid to say anything in case I said something that ruined everything.

'You're so cute,' she said, looking into my eyes, studying me with a curiosity that suggested she saw something other than my geeky face. 'I'll call you at six.'

She pushed her chair out with her bum, leaned across the table, brought the side of her face to the side of mine and whispered, 'I think I like you.'

Then she picked up her handbag and left. I stayed in my chair for the next ten minutes.

Chapter 3

Red Wine and Familiar Spirits

'Do not put your hand inside the finger. What does that mean?' Rachel said.

She turned the light purple paper around, and like everyone else who'd handled it she held it up to light to inspect it.

I was unable to concentrate on anything after I returned to the office from having coffee with Adesua. I was checking the time every ten minutes or less. It was driving me mad and I needed something to occupy my mind: something other than work. So I booked one of the glass-walled meeting areas and sent a meeting invitation to Rachel.

I'd written down the words of the letter onto a piece of paper I liberated from a printer. I was sure I remembered it exactly. My memory is good like that. Rachel read it first, before picking up the blank purple paper. I watched her closely. I still didn't know who wrote it, so everyone was a suspect.

'And you found it on your table?' she said.

'Yes. What are you thinking?'

She looked too serious about the letter to be one of the pranksters.

'I don't think it is a practical joke.'

'No? You think it's real?'

She looked at me as if what I said made her deeply disappointed in me.

'It's a scam,' she said.

'A scam? How?'

'I don't know. But this is 419. Maybe they'll ask you to pay them some money to join them, or they'll say your father left something valuable for you, or… I don't know. But I know it is a scam.'

'A scam?'

I thought about it as I looked at the blank purple paper. I shook my head.

'No. It is a prank. Someone in this office left the letter on my desk. If it was posted, I would agree that it could be a scam, but the envelope doesn't have a stamp.'

'So what? Letters are hand delivered to the office every day. A clerk could have collected it from the mail room and dropped it onto your table.'

'I just don't see how they can use it to scam me. I think it's someone in this office and I think the prank is to get me to believe someone is really going to teach me magic.'

I looked out through the glass wall at the expanse of the open plan office of the IT department. Maybe the perpetrators were watching Rachel and me scratching our heads over their pièce de résistance.

'You know it rained yesterday?' Rachel said.

'Yeah.'

'The letter said that rain must not beat you.'

'Yeah. So?'

'They are good. There used to be a scam, they would tell someone that they have a special liquid that they use to wash special paper into money. They will pour a little quantity of the liquid and wash some paper in front of the mugun and it would turn into money. Then they will say they need money to buy more special paper to wash into money. As a guarantee that they won't cheat the person, they will tell him to hold on to the remaining liquid while they go and use his money to buy more paper. Overnight, no matter how careful the mugun is, the glass container holding the special liquid would break. The next day, it is the mugun who is hiding from the fraudsters, thinking he has lost the extremely expensive special liquid they gave him to hold as surety for his money.

'Those kind of scam artists who know chemistry like that can easily make ink disappear on paper. I bet that it was predicted that it would rain yesterday and they were hoping the rain would have drenched you, then you would have believed them totally and you would think you had lost your chance to learn juju, and they would tell you there is a way for you to still learn it but it'll cost some money.'

It actually made sense. I felt stupid that I'd not come up with the theory myself.

'What should I do?' I said.

'You mean when Brother Amos contacts you?'

'It's Brother Moses.'

'Moses, Amos, whatever. Report him to EFCC.'

'What would I tell them?'

'That he's trying to dupe you.'

'But... I... The letter is blank. He can claim he never sent anything to me.'

'Mehn, these guys are good.'

<hr />

Adesua called at exactly six o'clock and asked if we could meet at the News Café at the Palms Mall. She said she had a meeting at Lekki phase one, so she could be there in ten minutes. It took me over forty minutes to get to Lekki Tollgate. She withheld her number when she called, so I couldn't call to tell her about the traffic that was bound to make me late. It was one of those Lagos traffic jams that, when you finally get through it, you can't see what caused it. An hour had passed since she called when I finally drove into Palms Mall. She had not called to ask where I was. I started to worry that if she wasn't in the News Café I wouldn't know if she had not yet arrived or if she had already left. To make matters worse, I had to switch off my AC because my car overheats in traffic, so I arrived with wet patches under my arms. My face was also shining like someone selling mango in the traffic jam.

Adesua was waiting for me at a table. She had bought a bottle of wine, which she had not touched. Two glasses were set on the table, one in front of her and one in front of the empty seat opposite her. She had seen me, so I couldn't sniff my armpits. I pinned my arms to my sides and walked over to her as if that was the way I normally walked.

She got up when I reached the table, and came and gave me a hug. I hugged her waist so that I didn't have to raise my hands and I ended up resting my hands on her bum. Idiot!

'The hold-up got you,' she said.

'Yeah. I'm sorry.'

'Don't be silly. It wasn't your fault.'

We sat and I noticed that there was a menu on my side of the table but not in front of her. The News Café is not the kind of place I normally go to buy food. I would never ever take a girl there unless I had just been paid a bonus. If she wasn't planning to eat, I would tell her I wasn't hungry either.

'I didn't have your number so I couldn't call you,' I said.

She looked as if she didn't understand.

'You withheld your number,' I explained.

Her face lit as she got my meaning, and she said, 'Sorry, I don't give my number out.'

Deflated. Wounded. Defeated. Humiliated. Oppressed. Embarrassed. All are words that cannot sufficiently describe how I felt at that moment. She held the serious look for a moment longer, then her face cracked into a tickled smile and she placed her fingers on my

33

forearm.

'I'm kidding,' she said. 'It's my company phone and I'm not meant to use it for personal stuff. I'll text you my personal number.

Be cool, Osaretin. Be cool. Breathe in. Breathe out.

'I got us wine,' she said. 'I'm not hungry. Are you?'

'Nope.'

She poured me a glass then she poured hers. She raised her glass for a toast.

'To us,' she said.

When I placed my glass back down, she said, 'So, tell me about Brother Moses. What happened?'

'Nothing yet. I think it could be a scam.'

'A scam? How?'

I was about to start presenting Rachel's theory as if it were mine when a waitress came to stand over us with her notepad ready to take orders.

'We're fine,' I said.

The waitress picked up the menu in front of me and knocked my glass over, spilling red wine all over the front of my shirt and my trousers, even as I jumped backwards trying to avoid the carnage. She dropped the menu and her notepad on the table and started using a handkerchief that had been in her back pocket to attempt to stop the wine dripping off the edge of the table, all the while saying, 'I'm sorry, sir. I'm sorry, sir.'

It was my white, long-sleeved Ralph Lauren Polo shirt. It was red wine. It pained me. I was beyond-beyond angry.

Adesua watched with a noticeable lack of excitement. It was almost as if the aftermath interested her more than the accident – which she had not reacted to either – and even then she looked more curious than interested.

'Put salt on it,' Adesua said. And to the girl, 'Can you get some salt, please? A lot of salt.'

The girl looked at Adesua. The two women stared at each other, neither one blinking or looking away.

The girl turned to me.

'Sir, we have special soap that we use to clean stains. If you go to the men's toilet and take off your shirt, I will quickly clean it and return it to you.'

Adesua placed her hand on my arm and spoke to the girl. 'It's fine. We are fine. Just get some salt.'

'Madam, we don't give salt for people to put on their clothes. If he gives me his shirt, I will clean it and dry it in less than fifteen minutes. We have a pressing iron I can use to dry it.'

I thought the girl was a bit rude, or it could have been her poor education that had deprived her of the vocabulary to say what she really meant to say without sounding the way she did. Nevertheless, I was soaked to the skin and preferred to take the shirt off and have it washed with their special soap rather than add salt to the mess. I didn't even believe the salt thing would work. It did seem strange that they had an iron for that very purpose. How often did they spill wine on their customers to warrant such preparedness? But I was more concerned with having my shirt cleaned than the café's laundry arrangements.

I told Adesua it would be fine. The girl followed me to the men's toilet. I handed the shirt out to her and went to pee. As I did so I wondered what I would do for the fifteen minutes she had promised it would take to clean the shirt. That was when I noticed the lines of text scribbled onto the wall in front of me. The most prominent line read: Beware of strange women. I read another: Keep your secrets secret. My eyes wandered to another: Do not rain on your own parade. I finished my business and was zipping up when another line caught my eyes:

Do not put your hand inside the finger.

I read every other line. I looked around for more. The other walls were devoid of such vandalism. The graffiti was only above the latrine I'd peed in. The remaining lines were:

Beware of familiar spirits

Do not lose your destiny because of what you will eat

Nothing in life is free. The price can be death!

To be warned is to be armed Test all spirits – 1 John 4:1

I read the alarming line again: Do not put your hand inside the finger. Was it a common saying I did not know? What did it mean? Did it mean anything?

A man entered the toilet and did a double take at my naked torso. 'I think there is a girl waiting for you outside,' he said.

Adesua had come to check on me. I checked myself in

the mirror, held my belly in, and stepped out of the toilet. It wasn't Adesua. It was the waitress who had spilled wine on me and she didn't have my shirt.

Instead, she spoke urgently and in whispers, looking about as she did so. She said: 'I intentionally poured the wine on you because I wanted to warn you that the lady with you has a familiar spirit.'

Chapter 4

A Storm Brewing Over Lagos

I returned to the café in my damp shirt. It was particularly uncomfortable around the collar and the sleeves. Maybe I should have given the waitress more time to iron it. But at least it was clean. I couldn't even tell where it had been stained.

Two men were seated at the table next to Adesua. A silver ice bucket holding a bottle of Dom Pérignon was on the table between them. They were looking at Adesua like thieves.

'She managed to get it all out,' Adesua said as I sat down.

'Yeah,' I said and noticed the waitress pointing me out to a man in blue trousers, pinstripe shirt, and a red tie. The man saw me looking and started marching towards me.

'Sir,' said the man, whose name badge also gave his job title as being the floor manager. 'Why were you shouting at my employee just now? Two customers have come to complain about how you spoke to her.'

The employee was standing behind her manager, looking neither offended nor guilty. I was put in a bad situation. I could say she stained my shirt, stop at that and have Adesua think of me as the type of person who talks down to people, or I could say what the girl said about Adesua and risk both upsetting Adesua, and getting the waitress fired. I chose a third option.

'I wasn't shouting at her,' I lied. I looked the girl in the eye, silently communicating how I was saving her ass and she had to save mine in return.

'You did not say,' he held up a notepad and read from it, 'Get out of my sight, you stupid illiterate. You are a fool. You are an imbecile. You are a nincompoop?'

I don't remember using those exact words but nonetheless Adesua gasped and her mouth remained opened as her eyes remained on me, seeing me in a new light.

'It wasn't like that,' I said to Adesua. 'It was a misunderstanding,' I said to the manager, and to the girl I said things in my mind that had I spoken out loud, the entire clientele of the bar, who were now looking at me, would have descended upon me as one big, righteous, lynch mob. 'It was just a misunderstanding. She spilled wine on me. It was not like that at all. It was a misunderstanding.'

The manager, realising he now had a larger audience who were no longer pretending not to notice, spoke louder, turning his head to this side then to that side so no one was left out, all the while keeping his eyes on me.

'We do not condone people insulting our staff at all,' he said. 'At all, at all. We do not accept that kind of rude behaviour here. Just because she is a waitress doesn't mean you can talk to her however you wish.'

Adesua's head was bent to the table. The other guests

were staring. The waitress was just standing there, and a hefty bouncer had left his post by the door and meandered over to the table. Then the manager went there, spitting out the words, 'Who do you even think you are?'

Now, I do not know what it is about those particular words that makes them a ubiquitous weapon of choice in every Nigerian fracas, and I do not know from where they acquired their strength to instantly escalate an already aggravated situation, but I reacted as predictably and as foolishly as any Nigerian would. I stood up, stepped up to my insulter, and inflated my body. Chest out, chin up, fists formed, arms held slightly out away from my body as if they could be called in an instant into active service and they needed space to manoeuvre.

'Look,' I began, then felt a heavy hand on my shoulder. I turned and gazed up at the huge bouncer. His face looked like he was pleading with me not to make him do what he would surely have to do.

'Ask her what she said to me,' I said. 'Go on, ask her. What did you tell me at the toilet?'

I already knew how it would go. She would remain mute, I would say what she said, she would deny every word, the bouncer would have to throw me out – maybe after punching me – and Adesua would melt away and I would never see her or hear from her again.

'I told him she is ogbanje,' the girl said, her hand stretched out and her finger rigidly pointing at Adesua.

The bouncer loosened his grip on me. The manager,

who had been about to speak, remained open-mouthed, the crowd gasped as one, and Adesua raised her head from the table.

'That's not all. After she said it, I told her to bring me my shirt and she said… ' I couldn't repeat it. 'Tell them what you said. Go on, tell them what you said.'

The girl just stood there silently, menacingly eyeing Adesua.

'Tell them,' I said, daring her to repeat her words. She remained silent. I looked around at the hitherto judging faces. I made eye contact with whomever I could. 'See?' my eyes were saying. 'See how it wasn't like you thought?'

The manager recovered enough to direct his invectives at the girl.

'What is wrong with you? Are you mad? How can you call our customers… You are a… Get out of my sight, you imbecile. I will deal with you later.'

The girl did not budge. Her eyes did not move from Adesua. She was tapping on the ground with one foot the way women in Nollywood movies do before they start pulling at each other's hair extensions. I felt I should move between her and Adesua. I saw the bouncer and the manager exchange looks, which somehow communicated that the bouncer should take the girl away. This girl, about five foot to the bouncer's seven foot, held up her fists to the approaching giant, like a boxer. That was when I realised she was mad.

The bouncer swatted her hands away, put his

over-muscular ones around her and lifted her off the ground. She kicked with her feet and the manager and I had to retreat.

'She is an evil spirit!' she screamed as the bouncer carried her away, kicking and spitting. Then, suddenly, everything went dark and silent. Not silent-silent – we could still hear the girl shouting from behind the back door she'd been carried through, and the murmur of the guests continued and was even more pronounced now that the music wasn't playing. But silent. Outside.

The entire bar lit for a brief second as the sky outside silently split open with lightning. Thunder did not follow.

From a nearby table someone observed of the black-out, 'It is everywhere.' They were looking out of the glass walls of the News Café at the high rises on the other side of the car park. They were right; it was not just the Palm Mall. Everywhere was dark and silent. People began to get up and go outside to investigate whether the blackout really covered the whole of Victoria Island. I was about to join them when suddenly all the car alarms went off. The sky lit up again. Fingers of lightning split the heavens and zigzagged to the corners of earth. The car alarms kept going. We all went outside. Everybody in Palm Mall came out onto the car park. Car owners pointed their keys at their vehicles, pressing buttons that did nothing. If you listened carefully, you could tell that it was not just the cars in Palm Mall. Car alarms were screaming from the estate to the left, the express road to the right, and the whole of Lekki to the rear.

Another silent shower of lightning fizzed across the sky. Adesua gripped my wrist so tightly that it hurt. I looked at her. She was frightened. She was looking at the sky. In another flash of light, I saw the extent of the horror on her face.

'They have started rolling the drum,' she said. Da wha'? Da who?

'What?' I said.

'We have to go.' She stepped forward and dragged me with her.

Other people were sensibly staying away from the cars. Adesua was running towards hers. And taking me with her.

'Adesua, I think we should wait till the storm is over.'

'It's not a storm,' she said.

She was strong. She walked quickly. I couldn't pull away from her grip and I had to almost jog to keep up with her.

'What do you mean it's not a storm?'

'I'll explain later.'

She stopped by a white Range Rover Sport. Without letting go of my hand, she opened the driver's door.

'Help me, sir,' a voice said from the ground. Behind us, between her Range Rover and a yellow Hummer, a cripple was on some sort of wooden board. His shriveled legs flapped from the sides of his belly that lay flat on the contraption. He raised one hand towards me and balanced

44

his irregular mass on the other. He was a beggar. He'd been caught in the storm. I instinctively reached down but Adesua slapped my hand away before I made contact.

'Don't touch him,' she said. 'He's a frog.'

Chapter 5

Lapu, Lapo, Laki

Adesua was superhumanly strong. She flicked her leg at the cripple, and with this gentle kick she propelled him five feet up into the air and at least twice as far away from us. With one hand, she lifted me into her car through the driver's door and placed me in a sitting position on the passenger seat. She leapt in and closed her door. Just as she did, I heard a thump on my window. I looked but couldn't see what it was. Just as I looked away, I heard it again. It sounded like someone was throwing something soft but heavy at us. I kept watching the window, waiting for the thump again. A frog leapt onto the glass. Thump! Its grey arms were spread, its white belly was against the glass, and it scraped with its legs as it tried to stop itself sliding off. I screamed, Adesua fired up the engine, revved loudly, and we screeched off.

She didn't slow down as she turned out of our lane onto the one between two rows of parked cars leading to the exit. My body pressed into my door. I expected the car to tip over onto its side. My side. I was grappling with the seatbelt when she tapped the throttle. The car lunged forward and my head slammed into the headrest. The sky lit up. Ahead of us, standing in the open gate, was the mad waitress from the bar. Adesua didn't slow down. The girl didn't move out of the way. I gripped the edge of my seat with my right hand, pushed the other hand against the dashboard, and pressed my foot down hard on a non-existent brake pedal in my footwell. We were a metre from hitting the girl when Adesua swerved left. This time I felt the wheels leave the ground. At lord knows what speed, we were suddenly facing the grinning grilles of a parked truck, and we'd run out of road.

———

I woke up and sat up. It was dark and silent. My body was damp with sweat. I was in my bed. It had all been a dream, but my heart was pounding hard nonetheless. It was a bad dream. I lay back down and tried to figure out what part was dream and what part was real. I was at the News Café, and Adesua was there. And we got into her car. I decided that much was real, but from that point on, everything must have been a dream. It was hot. There was a blackout, which meant no air conditioning as the landlord had recently told the caretaker not to start the generator after midnight. I got up, staggered, steadied myself, and went to open the window. I drew the curtain back and saw the sky light up. I let go of the curtain, stepped back and grimaced in anticipation of the thunder. It never came. Then I remembered the electrical storm. So that part had not been a dream. What else was not a dream?

Standing there in front of the curtain which was intermittently lighting up, I began to remember more of the dream and I steadily became confused because none of it felt like a dream, even though all of it was too strange to be real. I could not remember anything beyond the moment when we were about to crash into a massive truck and die. I couldn't remember Adesua dropping me at home. Had I been that drunk? Did I pass out in her car? If so, how did I give her directions to get to my place? Something strange was happening. Suddenly, I felt uncomfortable about the thunderless, rainless, windless electrical storm, about all those car alarms going off at once, about the state-wide blackout. What if it was not just Lagos wide? What if it was the whole of Nigeria? What if it was the entire planet?

As potently alarming as the thought was, I knew it couldn't be. It just couldn't be. If the storm was happening worldwide, and if it had caused the blackout, and that too was worldwide, that would mean something really, really bad was happening. That just couldn't be the case. The world could not be ending.

I went to leave the room. At the door I heard voices. I stopped and listened. The voices were coming from the tiny parlour of my one-bedroom apartment. Moving slowly, so that I would not be heard, I placed my ear to the door. My heart was beating so fast that it failed to keep a regular pattern and was doing more of a double-time random morse code rhythm. Had I left the door open? Had robbers got in? A male voice was speaking slowly and calmly, but I couldn't pick out anything he was saying. He did not seem to be speaking any language I'd heard before. It was not Edo, it was not Yoruba, it was not African sounding at all, nor did it sound European or Asian or Arab or even Latin. Through the plywood door the man's voice was muffled, and the sounds seemed like gibberish. 'Da da da da dum, da rum hum, la la da de. Lapu, lapo, laki.' And so it went on. Then, someone knocked on my bedroom door three times exactly where I'd placed my ear. I jumped. Adesua's voice said, 'You can come out any time you're ready.'

The man continued with his strange words 'Lapu, lapo, laki. Da da da, rum, da da da kum. Kapa, da da. Ru, ru, zoo la do la.'

Adesua spoke back to him. She spoke louder and with more force. The man replied to her angry voice with his calm 'da da's and she raised her voice even more. They were having an argument in their strange language.

I knocked on the door. They both stopped talking.

'Who are you?' I said.

Adesua replied, 'Me or he?'

'He.'

They had another brief exchange. The man next spoke to me: 'Master Osaretin, please do come and join us.'

He called me master. Was it Brother Moses? What the hell was going on?

I found my jeans and shirt on the chair by the bed. When I opened the door, it was not because I was less afraid. If the world was indeed ending, I wanted to be with other people, even if they seemed to have something to do with the brewing apocalypse.

They had lit a candle, stuck it to one of my plates, and placed it on a square stool in the middle of the room. Adesua was standing to the left behind the stool, and a bearded man was on the right. He was a couple of inches shorter than Adesua, who had taken off her shoes, and placed them on top of the stool, so that they lay along two edges, with the tips touching together at one corner.

The man was holding his own shoes in one hand. Purple brogues. That would have been strange if he was not also wearing a purple fedora, a purple corduroy jacket with huge lapels, the whitest shirt I'd ever seen with glass buttons that sparkled in the weak light of the candle, and baggy dark purple trousers that were striped with different shades of purple.

Adesua stared at me without the smile I'd come to expect from her. The man, on the other hand, was beaming. His face looked young in spite of the abundant grey streaks in his enormous beard.

'I am so very delighted to meet you at last,' he said. He carefully placed his shoes on the ground without taking his eyes off me, and slid his feet into them. He then took off his hat, stepped out from behind the stool, and extended his right hand to me. He had a huge afro.

I did not think it was safe to shake hands with him, so I kept mine firmly by my sides.

'Who are you?' I said. 'What are you doing here?'

'I am Brother Moses. We have an appointment. I sent you a letter.

'You are the one who sent the letter? The magician?'

'Yes, yes. The magician. And so are you, Master Osaretin.'

'I am not a magician. Magic is not real. Who are you? What do you people want from me?'

'Oh, magic is real, Master Osaretin, you just wait till we teach you some.'

'No. This is a scam. You are fraudsters. None of this is real. Who are you people? '

'I told you. We are magicians, just like you.'

'No. I am not like you. I am not a magician. I am not a fraudster. Who are you people? What do you want from me?'

'Magic is not real? How do you explain all of this?'

The entire living room lit up. The storm was real.

'How are you doing that?' I said. 'What is going on?'

'You tell me.'

'It is not magic.'

'Then what is it?'

The room lit up again.

'I don't know. I don't know what it is. I don't know how you're doing it.'

'Well, Master Osaretin, there is a name people use for things they cannot explain. But you do not believe. Not yet. And you are right, in a way. We are not the same. Not yet. You cannot imagine a world with magic. I cannot imagine a world without magic. But I was once like you. You see, Master Osaretin, we only know what we know until we know more.'

Adesua had been watching, but she did not appear to be interested in the conversation. She was merely witnessing something occurring in her immediate vicinity.

'Adesua, what's going on?' I said.

She turned her face away from me and spoke to Brother Moses in their strange language and in her angry voice. She was quite upset at him over something, but why was she ignoring me?

'What's going on?' I repeated.

Brother Moses answered me while Adesua stood and looked at me as if I was the reason she was upset.

'What you are witnessing is a syzygy,' he said.

'I don't speak your language,' I said.

'Oh, it's English. But yes, it is derived from Greek, syzygía. It's an alignment of three celestial bodies. In this case, it's the alignment of the Earth, the moon, and planet Bolanle.'

Bolanle is a girl's name in Yoruba. The man was obviously mad. Maybe the storm had affected his mind, driving him insane and making Adesua angry with him and cold toward me. Maybe they were both mad. That would explain the nonsense language I'd heard them speaking, and also what they had done with their shoes. Maybe it would start affecting me too, if it hadn't already.

'There is a planet called Bolanle?'

'Oh yes,' Brother Moses said. 'A planet called Bolanle? Yes, yes.'

'A planet called Bolanle?'

'Yes. And tonight it is aligned with the Earth and the moon.'

'And this alignment of the Earth, the moon, and the planet Bolanle is what is causing the storm?'

'No. Not exactly. The alignment is just a signal. People on different planets in the universe use these occurrences to synchronise events. This particular syzygy was agreed to be used as the signal for the commencement of a great event, and the signal has been noted on no fewer than half a dozen planets in our solar system alone.'

I saw his hair move. I'd not paid much attention to it till then, but the afro was at least six inches thick, and almost entirely white down the middle and the sides under his ears, leaving a stripe of black along each side of his head. As I watched his hair, it moved again. It was as if the hair were alive.

I couldn't stop myself from pointing at his undulating afro.

He looked confused for a moment before his face lit up and the keen smile returned. He gently patted his hair where it had bulged.

'Oh, that is Caesar,' he said.

He left his fingers on his hair and a red, yellow, and black snake came out of his hair and curled round his palm.

54

I cried out in horror and backed away, slamming into my bedroom door.

'What the hell is going on?' I shouted. 'Who the hell are you people? Who keeps a snake in their hair? What the hell is this?'

I think the word for my state at that moment was 'hysterical'. A smiling, unperturbed Brother Moses, held the snake hand out in front of him and began walking towards me.

⁂

I woke suddenly and sat up in bed. It was dark. It was silent. A moment passed and I realised I'd had one of those dreams in which you dream that you wake from a dream, not realising that you have only woken up in the second dream and you are still dreaming the first dream in which you'd dreamt that you were dreaming.

It was hot. I had slept in my clothes. I got up to go and open the window and I saw the sky light up silently with a storm that had no thunder. I heard voices coming from my living room. 'Du, da da, ra lo, ra ra. Lapu, lapo, laki.'

I began to cry.

Chapter 6

A Coin in Time

In my living room there's space for a two-seater sofa and a fuchsia tub chair that I acquired when the IT department waiting room was being refurbished. I learnt both the name of the armchair and its colour from Rachel, who took home its twin. I sat in the chair by the door to my bedroom and faced Adesua and Brother Moses, who were sitting opposite me, side by side, without space to spare on the small sofa. Between them and me was the stool, atop which their shoes were now arranged so that the heels were at the corners and the toes all pointed at the candle in the middle.

I'd knocked and waited before entering my own living room. In that time they must have seated themselves on the sofa to appear less terrifying.

We sat in this fashion, eyeing each other across the steady tongue of the candle's flame. Adesua's face was unwavering, with no hint as to what she may have been thinking, while Brother Moses continued to beam his merry smile at me as if it were a happy occasion. I scrutinised his hair for movement but detected none.

'He's gone,' he said. He leaned forward and bowed his head, offering me the assurance of checking for myself.

If the snake was no longer there, where was it? I drew my feet onto the armchair.

'No, no, no.' Brother Moses said. 'Caesar is no longer here. What did you do with it?'

'Do with it? Nothing. He was upsetting you so I told him not to come out again.'

'Out from where? Is it still in your hair?'

'Yes and no.'

'Yes and no? Which is it?' I returned my feet to the carpet, but my skin continued to anticipate the cold brush of a phantom snake.

'Caesar lives in my hair, along with some other pets. I also keep other useful things in there. Have you ever seen a stairoscope?'

'What do you mean, lives in your hair?'

'Oh, I forgot, you have not yet been initiated. I will explain. You know of three dimensions, but there are others in between, like corridors. Some of these are called folds. I've mastered how to use these folds to hide things. It is the mastery of these dimensions that is the source of most magic.'

He interpreted the look on my face as disbelief. I just didn't know what to think.

'Have you ever dropped a coin and immediately searched for it and not found it? That's because the coin, quite by accident, has fallen into a fold. At a later date you might find the coin in a place you have searched before and you might wonder who put it there. Has this ever happened to you?'

'No. We don't use coins in Nigeria.'

'Oh, I forgot what year it is. Ok, ok. Maybe a ring, or a button that comes loose on your shirt. It has to be something relatively small like that, to increase the chances of slipping through the fold. I have already told you the secret of this dimension. Did you pick up on what it is?'

He expected me to know something. I stared back at his smiling face and said nothing.

'Time!' he said. His excitement did not travel. He was mad. But where was the snake?

'You think of time as linear. But what if time is constant, fixed, finite, and it is one or all of the other dimensions that are dynamic?'

In the glow of the candlelight, his smiling face awaited my response.

'Who are you people and what do you want from me?'

'We are magicians, like your father. Like you.'

'My father was not a magician, he was a doctor.'

'He taught you some magic, though. Do you still remember it?'

'Tricks. He did tricks. He was a doctor. You have the wrong person. Please, just go. Just leave me alone.'

Adesua turned to Brother Moses. 'What did I tell you? He's useless. We shouldn't have bothered.'

Brother Moses ignored her.

'You are a magician, Master Osaretin. It is in your blood. Let me show you. He fetched an object from an inner pocket of his jacket. It was a wooden cube, about three inches square. He held it between his thumb and middle finger and offered it to me across the stool. I stayed where I sat. 'Do you know what this is?' he said. 'Do you know what it does? Do you recognise it? Did you play with one like it when you were a kid?'

I shook my head. In case he didn't notice in the poor light, I said, 'No. I don't know what it is.'

'Think. Try to remember. Your father gave you one when you were little.'

'No. I've never seen it before.' I recalled building blocks, but I wasn't going to encourage him.

'Try to remember. Look at it. What does it do?'

Adesua spoke. 'It's useless. He's not the one. I told you.'

'She's right,' I said. 'You have the wrong person. Please, just leave me alone.'

Brother Moses returned the cube to his pocket. For the first time, the smile left his face, but only for the time it took him to fetch a coin, toss it, and catch it in the air. He hid the coin under his right palm over the back of his left hand.

'Heads or tails?' he said.

I shook my head.

'Please try, Master Osaretin. Heads or tails?'

'I don't know.'

'Guess, Master Osaretin. Guess.'

'I don't want to guess.'

60

'Useless,' Adesua said.

I looked at her. Her face was blank. Maybe the disappointment, impatience, disgust, and many other forms of loathing were all cancelling each other out.

The room lit up. This time it wasn't the silent storm. Power had returned. The world hadn't ended. The nightmare was over. Yet two of its actors remained.

Adesua looked at the single shaded light bulb hanging from my ceiling and then she looked at Brother Moses, who looked back at her. I looked out of the window. The steady darkness of the sky had never been such a source of joy. With the return of normalcy I gained confidence.

'I've had enough of your games. Just tell me who are you and what you want from me.'

Brother Moses didn't look so otherworldly in the light. He was just a madman dressed in purple.

'Master Osaretin. Your father used to toss a coin and make you guess which way it landed. He also used to balance a coin on a device similar to the one I showed you. He was teaching you things to prepare you for this day. Do you want to know how he made the egg disappear?'

He got me. It showed on my face.

'Yes, Master Osaretin. Your father could catch an egg in the air the way I caught this coin, and it would vanish in his palm. He never showed you how he did it, or how he made money appear in his handkerchief.'

'How do you know that? There is no way you can possibly know that.' I was afraid again. 'How do you know about my father?'

'We were friends. I can tell you many things about him but you wouldn't believe me unless you first accept that he was a magician and so are you.'

'We are wasting time,' Adesua said.

'No. Master Osaretin will remember. It is in you, Master Osaretin. You are a great magician, just like your father. Tell me about my father.'

The smile returned to his face. He rested his back against the sofa and began.

'It was the winter of 1975, and my beard was in full bloom.'

Chapter 7

The Prefiguration of Mr Magic

'We met at a Jazz Club in Soho. He was in London attending a medical convention and I had just moved to the city, as I was due to begin a degree in Theology at King's College.

'I was playing a trick on a French lady I'd met earlier in Trafalgar Square. I presented my beard to her and invited her to pour a glass of wine into it. Efosa was watching. After the trick, he came to our table and asked if he could also pour his water into my beard. I told him he couldn't but he poured it all the same and made my clothes wet. Everyone who'd seen me do my trick laughed at what he'd done, including the girl, but I alone knew that although he had poured only a small cup of water into my beard, more than a bucketful passed through and soaked my clothes.

'I was only Magnificent, but he was Grand. He was a Most Grand Magician of the First Order. To become Grand you have to master all the other dimensions. Efosa had mastered them all. Only few ever become Grand. For them, magic comes naturally. It is in their blood. There is no trick performed by any magician that they cannot duplicate. They can also ruin a lesser magician's trick, like he ruined mine.

'To become something even greater than Grand, you have to discover a new dimension that no one else knows about. In this way, no other magician will be able to recreate your tricks. People said Efosa had discovered such a dimension.'

My phone began to ring in my trouser pocket, strengthening my suspicion that I had not undressed myself before I woke up naked in bed. But who could be calling at three in the morning?

'Who is it?' Adesua said.

They were both looking at me. The ringing phone had made them uncomfortable. I checked the name on my screen.

'It's my workmate, Rachel.'

'Don't answer it.'

'Why not?'

She didn't reply, but before I could answer the phone Brother Moses said, 'You must really like women a lot.'

'Why?' I asked, affronted

'Because they keep using women to try to catch you.'

'What do you mean?'

The phone stopped ringing. A few seconds later the message alert beeped.

'Read it out,' Adesua said.

I defiantly refused to follow Adesua's instructions, but I gave them the gist of what is said. 'She's on her way here.'

Adesua stood up.

'We must leave now,' she said.

'No,' Brother Moses said. 'Let her come. Let him see for himself.'

I didn't know what on earth they were talking about, but I was spooked. They were spooky. What had Rachel got to do with any of this?

Adesua sat back down. 'Are you sleeping with her?' she said. I wanted to lie that I was.

'No. But she likes me.'

We were more like best friends. We even referred to one another as brother and sister and meant it.

She sniggered. She looked at Brother Moses. Brother Moses shook his head at her and spoke to me.

'We don't have much time. I must tell you something quickly. I won't be able to explain all of it now, but you'll understand everything later. Your father told me about a magician who was born with knowledge of all dimensions known and yet to be known. He said that he was afraid of this magician. Your father, who had explored the dimensions of infinite fear until he became bored, was afraid of this character. He said that this magician had discovered the so-called God Dimension, and once he mastered it, he would have the power to destroy all of creation and recreate it in any way he desired. This is why we have come for you.'

'What has it got to do with me?'

Adesua answered me. 'He thinks you are the one.'

'Me?' I asked. She sounded like she didn't believe it. Maybe she wasn't insane after all.

Brother Moses had a forlorn look on his face. 'Yes, I'm afraid so. Your father never said who it was, but he told me his performance name, Mr Magic. I asked every magician I knew but no one else had heard of him except your father. In time I came to realise it was you, and he was only trying to protect you.'

'Protect me? From what?'

'From the people coming to get you now.'

My phone rang again. It was Rachel. Adesua and Brother Moses watched me as I held the ringing phone in my hand, unsure what to do.

'Answer it,' Brother Moses said. 'But whatever you do, do not invite her in.'

I answered the phone. 'Hello?'

'Osaretin, oh my God, I'm so happy to hear your voice. Did you get my message?' Rachel said.

'Yes.'

'I'm downstairs.'

'Okay.'

'Have you watched the news?'

'No.'

'It was a solar flare. It's on CNN. It affected the whole world. It bathed the entire globe in a plasma cloud. It disrupted everything electrical. They said it's a new kind of phenomenon that has never been experienced before. They are carrying out tests to determine whether it has had any lasting effects. As far as they know, everything has returned to normal and no lives have been lost.

'I was really, really scared, Osaretin. I thought the world was going to end and the only person I kept thinking of was you. I just wanted to be with you. I'm at your door now. Please let me in.'

'You are at the door?' I said, looking at Adesua and Brother Moses.

'Yes. Let me in.'

The doorbell rang and I jumped.

I knew it was Rachel on the phone. It was her voice. But I was afraid to open the door.

'Rachel,' I said. 'What colour was the paper I showed you?'

She did not answer. She knocked on the door.

'Rachel? What colour is my tub chair?'

She banged on the door.

'Rachel?'

'Let me in right now!'

I ended the call, dropped the phone on the chair and got to my feet.

The banging continued. The entire door shook in its frame.

'Don't worry,' Brother Moses said. He was so calm. He wasn't even looking at the door.

'They can't come in if you don't invite them.'

'They?'

'Yes. It is not your friend. I suspect there's at least two of them. They won't take chances with a magician like you.'

'Who are they?'

'They are also magicians. They want to use your powers to destroy many universes.'

The banging stopped. What was out there?

'Why?'

'I can't explain now, we don't have time.'

A thought suddenly filled me with hope.

'What year was it when my father told you about this Mr Magic?' I held my breath.

'1975.'

'Don't you see? It can't be me. I wasn't born then!'

I knew it. They had the wrong person. I wanted to share the information with whoever was out there hoping I'd let them in.

'It was a prophesy,' Brother Moses said. 'Few magicians learn this trick. Anyone who knows how to can travel back and forth in time, but whatever information they bring back from the future is useless because they have observed it, and in so doing, altered it. Efosa was one of the few magicians who could return from the future and leave the future intact.

'He could prophesy things to come. He predicted your birth and your powers. He talked about you as if you were already a grown man, so that others would not know who you are. He told me all I needed to know so that I would realise it was you.'

'But what if you are wrong?'

'What you witnessed tonight in the sky, that was them

trying to find you. They used a device called the drum. Its use on this planet is unprecedented. No. I lie. It has been used once before – they were looking for someone they wished to crucify. It's like a radar that can scan an entire planet.'

'What were they scanning for?'

'For a magician with your powers.'

'I have no powers.'

'You do. You just don't know it yet.'

'What if they used their scanner to find you, and then they simply followed you to me? Is that a possibility?'

'Yes,' Adesua said.

'No,' Brother Moses said.

'Can we leave now?' Adesua said. She looked bored.

'He must want to come with us,' Brother Moses said. 'It must be his choice. Master Osaretin, will you come with us?'

Chapter 8

Always Coming When You're Going

I was on my feet. Adesua and Brother Moses were waiting for my decision. Time ticked away in its linear direction.

'I need to pee,' I said.

'We don't have time,' Adesua said.

'I'm coming,' I said, and I went into my room and shut the door behind me. My brain was working faster and harder than it had ever done before. So far I had not witnessed anything extraordinary enough for me to start believing in magic. Brother Moses did produce a snake from his afro, but in the dim light how could I be sure of what I saw? And the silent storm was a solar flare. But it was Rachel who had told me this, and they claimed she wasn't the one outside.

I went to the window. Rachel's car was outside, three floors down. I could see her through her windshield. She was making a call and waiting for it to be answered. I'd left my phone in the living room.

It could still all be a scam, but it would be the most elaborate scam ever, hardly worth anything they could get from me. There was something happening, but I just didn't know what it was.

I had to make a decision. To believe them would be

to suspend all logic, something I'd never managed to do, hence my inability to find a Nigerian girl interested in me, as most of them believe that atheists are evil. I no longer bothered to explain that I'm actually agnostic.

On the weight of evidence, Adesua and Brother Moses were mad, and should I continue to listen to them, or to follow them, I would run the risk of being infected with their madness. I was sure they believed what they said, and I was worried that soon they'd have me believing it too.

A year ago my neighbour locked himself out of his flat. He knocked on my door and asked if he could climb out of my bedroom window to his. He managed it without falling. After that I stopped leaving my bedroom window open when I was out.

I pulled the curtains fully apart then slid the one movable glass pane all the way across. I poked my head out to see just how far it was to the adjoining window. Like my neighbour, I would have to first climb onto the ledge that ran beneath both our windows, then, with one hand still safely tethered to my own window, I would reach out to his, get a good grip, then hoist myself over. Leaning out further, I could see that his window was open. I looked down. I looked at his window again. I raised my left leg and put it through my open window.

<hr>

Brother Moses was on his side of the sofa. His shoes

were also on the stool but Adesua and her shoes were gone.

'Where is she?' I said.

'She went to catch you in case you fell.'

'Oh.'

I shut my bedroom door and sat back down in the tub chair.

'You are not really playing your cards right with her,' he said. Cards? I didn't realise I had cards.

'Magicians get the prettiest girls,' he said, 'and girl magicians always go for magicians.'

What was that he said about always using girls to trap me? 'In your letter you said I shouldn't know a woman,' I said.

'Yes. It is one of the requirements. Did you know a woman?'

'No. But Adesua and I…'

I left it to his magician head to complete the sentence.

'Oh no, no, no, no, no. She would never have. She merely made sure you wanted to be with her so much that you wouldn't have any thought for another woman. She cast a spell on you, you see. One of the oldest tricks.'

I nodded and tried not to show that a dagger had found my heart.

'She doesn't like me,' I said.

'It's not personal.'

'She doesn't think I'm the one.'

'It doesn't matter what she thinks.'

73

'Where do you want to take me?'

'To meet a great magician.'

'Where is that?'

'Not far from here.'

Adesua returned. She entered my flat as if she lived there. Her eyes swept over me like I was of no consequence. Was that even her name, Adesua? Was she really also Edo? Was she really a woman?

'They are still out there,' she said.

Brother Moses stood up and offered me his hat.

'Use this,' he said. 'It will disguise you for just long enough.' Was that where he hid the snake?

Back in my bedroom, halfway out of the window and halfway from certain death, it had occurred to me that my choices were as sparse as they were obvious: follow them or tell them to get the hell out. I hadn't considered the second option until I looked down from the very different perspective of having half my body out the window.

'I don't want to come with you,' I said.

'Fine,' Adesua said. She turned to leave but Brother Moses placed his arm on her shoulder.

'I was really hoping I wouldn't have to do this,' he said. He placed his hat upturned on the stool.

Do what? I wondered.

'We are travelling magicians,' he said, 'we are performers, just like you father, and that is where your training will begin as well. There is a dimension in which all things are possible. The way to access this dimension is through the imagination of others. As performers, it is our job, our desire, our reward, to astonish and mesmerise our audience through our magnificent and grand tricks. Whenever we accomplish this, be it in a child witnessing magic for the first time, or in the hearts of curious pedestrians gathered round a street magician, we unlock that most inaccessible of dimensions:we make them believe, if only for a short while. We make them dream.

'I cannot make you believe, Master Osaretin. You must do that on your own. And it has to be true faith. That is why I can't show you any of my top ten tricks which, I assure you, my soul itches to reveal. But I can give you this.'

He held out an object which I had not seen him take out of any of his pockets or his hair. It was a silvery sphere about an inch in diameter. He held it between the tips of his thumb and index finger. My living room curved around its tiny surface.

'What is it?' I asked. My hands remained by my sides.

'I am leaving you my hat, to disguise your appearance if you need it, but just in case you are rumbled and they catch you, use this to get back to this place at this time.'

'How do you mean?'

'It's like a recorder. I have just set it to start recording from a few moments ago. It stops recording and rewinds to when it started when you use it. Take it. I hope you won't have to use it.'

What harm could a tiny steel ball do? I held out my

palm and he placed the object in it. My hand dropped and I had to bend and use my other hand to support the hand with the ball in it. It was as if he had handed me a tome of a book. It was not that heavy, to be fair, but in relation to its size its weight took me by surprise. It was as heavy as, say, a big dictionary.

'It gets heavier the more it records,' Brother Moses said. 'The same conditions from the letter still hold. It will be difficult for you to keep the women off, but you must resist and remain focused for your initiation.'

Adesua opened the door and left my flat without a word, a nod, or even a bad-eye look – which for me would have been better than the way she totally ignored me.

At the door Brother Moses stopped and turned round.

'When you went to your room to jump, you said, 'I am coming'.'

'I wasn't going to jump. I was...' If he didn't know, he could leave with his condescending conclusion.

'You said you were coming. Do you remember? Just before you left, you said, 'I'm coming."

'Yes. So?'

'I am coming. That is what you said, even though you were leaving.'

I'd never thought about it till then, but when he pointed it out, for the first time I realised it must be a Nigerian thing, like dressing well which meant moving over on a bench so someone else can fit in. I thought of all the times I'd left a place and said, 'I'm coming.' I shrugged off the pointless embarrassment. Everybody says it, anyway.

'No. Not everybody. Just the people of a particular tribe and the people who have had dealings with them and learnt their ways. See you soon, Master Osaretin. I am leaving now.'

I shut my door. I did the locks. I prodded his hat with the end of my TV remote control and I admired the un-usually heavy tiny ball before putting it into my pocket. Then I realised he hadn't told me how to use it.

Chapter 9

Osmium or Not

I have long suspected that the mind must not be trusted in the hours between bedtime and dawn.

After Adesua and Brother Moses left, I remember yawning so long and with my mouth so wide open that I felt the muscles of my jaw straining. It was late, I was tired, and I had to get some sleep because the world had not ended and there was work in the morning.

It was the most peaceful, dreamless, sweet sleep I've ever had: one of those rare times that you fall asleep as soon as your head touches the pillow. Literally. And when I woke up I was refreshed. I got less than four hours sleep and I woke up totally alert, feeling well rested and full of life. I even woke up before the alarm.

As I took my shower, I reflected on the amazingness of the last few hours, how sleep deprivation had led me into a world of magic and portable time machines and magicians with stage names like Mr Magic.

Lack of sleep, those mysterious early hours, and the sheer lure of the fantastic yarn of Adesua and Brother Moses had made it all seem plausible. In the morning, however, I remembered it as what it truly was; two professional scammers who wanted something from me that required me to believe I was a magician. Mr Magic. I laughed, and right then I realised what it was. They wanted to rob the bank and they needed me in some way to carry out their heist. It was plausible. They needed an inside man. They had planned for me to be him. Mr Magic my foot. I had rumbled them.

But, coming down from my mini-euphoria, I found that I was missing the strange and pretty girl, Adesua. And when I passed the purple hat on my way out, harmlessly immobile on the stool, I thought of the smiling Brother Moses with a fondness that surprised me.

<hr />

'Where is it?' Rachel said.

I had booked a meeting for both of us in one of the glass meeting rooms. We had little to do, anyway; the head of IT had asked the infrastructure team to carry out an inspection of all systems to determine whether the solar flare had compromised anything. The head of infrastructure had sent out an email informing all staff that they were not to do anything on the network until he gave the all clear. As a result, all members of staff who did not know how to configure a router were using social media on their phones or sharing stories about the previous night with their colleagues.

I scanned the open plan office before removing the sphere from my pocket.

'Let me see.'

She held her palm out.

'It is very heavy,' I said.

I placed my free palm under hers and put the sphere in her hand.

'Wow. You are right. It's heavy.'

I took my hand away from under hers and she tested the weight of the sphere.

'It is really heavy,' she said, as if she hadn't believed me.

She placed it onto the glass surface of the stool between us. It landed with a clank so loud I feared the glass would break, then it rolled about an inch and stopped. She picked her phone from the stool and started punching at its keyboard. She looked up from the screen, looked down at the sphere, then looked back at her screen. Her face showed that she had discovered something.

'It is osmium,' she said.

She showed me what she had found on the internet. Osmium (from the Greek osme (ὀσμή) meaning 'smell'), element symbol Os, atomic number 76. A hard, brittle, bluish-white transition metal in the platinum group, blah blah blah. Densest naturally occurring element, with a density of 22.59 g/cm3. The picture on her phone, of a rough roundish metallic lump, was not the same as my perfectly spherical, polished ball.

'Osmium. That sounds radioactive,' I said.

'I don't think it is. Have you weighed it?'

I hadn't thought of doing that. For a second in the

81

morning, when I'd forgotten about the ball in my pocket and I was putting on my trousers, I did think it weighed more than it had when Brother Moses first gave it to me. But just as quickly I concluded that it was only in my mind because Brother Moses had said it would get heavier. I wasn't sure any more.

'You mean to see if it gets heavier?' I said.

Rachel gave me a 'don't be stupid' look. 'No,' she said. 'I just want to know how heavy it is.'

She picked it up into her palm and brought it to her nose to sniff, then she set it back down on the stool, this time by placing her palm down and gently tipping it sideways to allow the sphere to roll off. It still made an even louder clank when it touched the glass. It rolled all the way to the edge, where the metal rim stopped it.

I saw Daniel walking towards us. He was the head of digital security, the only white man in the IT department. He was British, and he liked Rachel, which made me think he didn't like me because a lot of people just didn't believe there wasn't something between us. He opened the door without respect for the fake meeting we could be having and said, 'Osa, they're looking for you upstairs.'

Upstairs could mean many things. On the sixth floor, directly above the IT floor was where we had the servers, above that were the IT service desk and training rooms, and above that was the main IT meeting room and the offices of the IT heads of this and that, including Daniel.

He walked ahead of me. He said, 'What were you guys

82

talking about?'

'Nothing. We had a meeting.'

'Yeah, I know you booked a meeting. That's how I found you. What was it about?'

'We are just catching up on some stuff.'

'Yeah? Stuff like?'

He swiped his card on the reader and held the door open for me. I headed towards the stairs at the end of the corridor, but he stood in the middle of the elevators on both sides. I walked back and stood next to him. He hadn't pressed a button, so I did.

'We've been going over access logs to see who was in the building doing what during the flare,' he said. 'We don't have anything from during the event, but we can see who last went through a door before and after it. I've been looking at tapes from the lobby.'

A lift, one of the four on each side of the corridor, opened. It was going up and it was empty. We got inside and he pressed 9. I wondered what I'd been caught doing. Not that I was aware of something I'd done, but it sounded like 'they' wanted to see me because they had discovered something I had done that I shouldn't have.

He didn't say anything during the short elevator ride. He used his access card to let us into the open plan workspace off of which meeting rooms and private offices radiated. He walked round the perimeter of silent face-to-monitor workers and used his card on his own office door. I'd been there once, to answer a query about lending my pass card to a colleague who had left his at home and needed to pop into the toilet.

'Sit,' he said.

I sat. He walked behind his desk, plucked his laptop from its power cable and brought it round to me. He set the computer in front of me, opened it up, and sat on the other chair meant for his guests. I still hadn't figured out what I'd done and that made me even more apprehensive. His tanned, hairy hand stretched across in front of me to get to the power button and I realised what it was. It was when I went downstairs to the banking floor and went behind the counters. Unauthorised access. This would be my second yellow card.

The screen lit up to a still image of the lobby downstairs as captured by one of the cameras directed at the elevators.

'I saw this from this morning,' he said. He clicked a button, and the seconds of the frozen time counter on the bottom left of the screen began to run.

I watched. I was sick to the belly by this time. I recognised myself walking into the shot. I'd never seen myself from that angle, from the top.

'This.' He paused the video as the elevator door opened and I stepped in.

What was I meant to see?

He drew his fingers across the touchpad on the laptop. He opened another video file. Again I saw myself getting into an elevator from the ground floor.

'That was yesterday.'

He clicked open another video. Again, I waited for the lift to arrive and, when it did, I got into it.

'There are eight lifts. Two buttons, one on each side, to call any of the lifts. Each time you arrive, you press a button then you stand in front of the lift that's going to open next.'

He clicked upon yet another video.

'You're a consistent chap. You arrive at 6:45 every morning. This one is from last month. See all those people bunched together there in front of one lift? But you, you are standing alone, in front of a different lift. Watch what happens. Your lift opens. The one you picked.

'I've gone downstairs to check. The lights over the lifts don't tell which is arriving next. There's no sound you might be listening to. I phoned the company that manages them; there's no pattern to which lift comes first. How do you do it?'

Chapter 10

Running Out of Time

'You have E.S.P. It means extrasensory perception. You have a sixth sense.'

Daniel played video after video, watching with excitement, and looking at me each time with a look that was expectant and thrilled and friendly all at the same time. He had never been friendly to me.

I, for my part, watched myself repeatedly arriving on his screen and stepping into lifts. Goosebumps crept over my body, and the back of my neck felt exposed to an axeman's aim. Fear permeated my entire being. Daniel continued talking excitedly about his discovery, he continued showing me the videos as if to convince me. He brought out his wallet and from it brought out a coin. It was a fifty pence coin. I'd never seen one till then. He tossed it and palmed it onto the back of his left hand. 'Heads or tails?' he said.

It all came back. Ever since I could remember, my father would toss a one kobo coin and tell me to guess heads or tails. He never showed me which it was and he never checked himself. Sometimes, after I'd picked a face he would say, 'concentrate,' and would ask me to guess again, but mostly he just tossed the coin again. He played this 'game' with me all the time, for hours on end, or so it seemed to me, a child who just wanted to watch cartoons. And at the end of the game I did not understand, he always seemed pleased with me, as if I'd done something right. Ever since I was a child.

'Heads or tails,' Daniel said, but the only thought in my perfectly terrified heart was the sphere: it was with Rachel. I had to get it back.

I left the ninth floor and, compelled by habit, pressed the button to call the lift. I took my finger away but it was too late, I'd done it. I looked up at the camera watching me. I hurried to the door that led to the stairs. I didn't want to hear the lift opening and find out which one came first.

My heart beating hard and fast with fear and anxiety and confusion, I flew down the stairs two steps at a time, pursued and propelled by a strong feeling of being in imminent danger.

I saw Rachel's head above her monitor. Would I tell her about the lifts? What would I say? I had already told her a lot. Had I put her in danger as well? I mean, she already knew... Well, she knew everything. She knew about the letter, about Adesua, Brother Moses, his hat, the snake, the sphere. She had touched the sphere. She had smelt it – breathed it into her lungs! I had to protect her. But how, and from whom?

Rachel looked up and saw me looking at her. I continued to her desk. I must not involve her any further in whatever was going on. Even at that moment, I realised that the only way to protect her was to get far away from her. It was me they wanted.

I passed Ade standing over Moyo's desk. They were the only open lovers in the office. Ade saw me approaching, smiled and nodded, looked at his watch and said to his lover, 'Time is moving really fast today.'

I stopped walking. I looked at him and asked, 'What did you say?'

He showed me his watch face and said it again, 'Time is moving really fast today.'

I checked my own watch. It was already midday. But how could that be? I arrived at work, sent Rachel a meeting invite and waited for her to arrive, showed her the ball, went upstairs to the ninth floor and came back down. It should be not a second more than ten. Fearful foreboding swept over me. Only I knew what was happening. I was literally running out of time!

Before I could say anything, Rachel said: 'Hey, I was thinking. These guys told you they want you to come with them because there are bad people who want you to go with them too, right? That is stupid. Think of it. If all their nonsense is true, how would you know that they are not the bad guys trying to stop you from joining the good guys?'

'What? Never mind. Listen, can I have the ball?'

'Your ball? You have it.'

'No. You have it.'

'Didn't you take it from the room?'

'No. I thought you did.'

I turned and she stood and we both looked at the meeting room we'd used. The room had at least seven people in it, our colleagues, all standing round the head of project management who was talking to them. She was known for long meetings.

I had to get my ball. I started walking to the meeting room not quite sure what I would do. I was aware of Rachel following me but maybe, if I ignored her, she'd go away. I stood before the meeting room and tried to see between the legs of the people in there, whether the sphere was still there. Their backs were to me but the head of project management saw me and gave me a questioning look. I looked away from her eyes and continued trying to see the top of the stool.

'Can you see it?' Rachel said.

I had to get rid of her for her own sake. I ignored her. She nudged me. She nodded and I looked. Daniel was on the floor and coming for me.

'Rachel,' I said, 'please go to your desk.'

'What did he want from you?' she asked.

'I'll tell you later, just go. Please. Now.'

She was still standing by my side when Daniel got to us. He was holding up his fifty pence coin, his face awash with the beam of yet another discovery, I feared. And I was right.

Heaving once before he spoke, as if he'd been doing

90

something strenuous, he began, 'I know why you didn't get it right. I said heads or tails, but you guys don't use coins in Nigeria, so you didn't know which side was the head and which side was the tail. Do you know the odds of getting it wrong ten times out of ten? It's the same as getting it right ten times out of ten. You were calling the correct side, you just didn't know it. And it wasn't ten times out of ten; it was more like twenty-five times out of twenty-five.'

He thought I did not know heads from tails. Because I was Nigerian. His condescension grated my soul – almost as badly as when he felt the need to tell me what E.S.P. was. I was starting to hate him – probably first for discovering my secret, and then for showing it to me, then for coming to confront me with it in front of someone I was trying to protect from this... this magic. But at that precise moment I hated him with an intensity approaching tipping point because he had rumbled me. I had intentionally called the wrong side each time he tossed his coin. I did it to throw him off. It upset me that he wasn't fooled for long. It upset me that I hadn't thought it through and got some right. It terrified me that I was able to intentionally get it wrong all the time.

'What is he talking about?' Rachel said.

I wished he would just go away and not stand there beaming at me as if we were new BFFs.

'He's got superpowers,' he said. 'He can predict stuff.'

Just then, the squeaky voice of the head of project

management screamed over the shouts and gasps of the others in the meeting room, and the sound of glass crashing onto marble tiles. We all turned. The stool's glass top was on the floor, directly beneath the frame, shattered into pieces like a glass jigsaw. I searched the ground for my sphere.

Rachel shouted, 'The ball!'

Chapter 11

The Other Men in Black

There ought to be a word for when everything occurs simultaneously in a momentary convergence of events in time and space, unified by all of these events happening to the same subject. At the exact same moment that my ball became too heavy for the glass, two white men in black suits, black ties, black shoes and white shirts, who had arrived at the lobby downstairs a few minutes earlier escorted by a major in the Nigerian Army and four of his soldiers wielding AK-47s, were given access to the sixth floor by the head of IT, who kept looking at the guns.

Without thinking, I entered the meeting room and forced my way between my colleagues who were all looking down at the glass top that had inexplicably shattered, apparently without impetus. I crouched before the broken pieces and searched for my ball. It seemed to have stopped where it landed, directly beneath the edge of the stool where it had rolled to before. I reached for it and felt an arm on my shoulder. Looking up, I was staring into the barrel of an assault rifle, which was so menacing that the body of the person holding it appeared out of focus behind it.

Frozen in place by a force emanating from the gun, I

waited to be told what to do.

'Are you Mr Osaretin Osagiemwenagbon?' a voice said. It didn't belong to the holder of the gun. I placed my extended hand onto the broken pieces of glass to support my body as I dared to swivel to see who had mispronounced my name with an American accent.

He was tall and slim. His face was rigid, with the practised lack of emotion worn by the military. His hair was blond, shaved at the sides, and swept forwards in a uniform inch of growth on the top. The other white man by his side was short and stout, his black suit unbuttoned, or unbuttonable due to his large belly, over which his tie rested like a drunk leaning on a bar. His head was shiny bald on top with a shock of curly brownish-orange hair on the sides. He had a pair of round wire-framed glasses, and his face looked friendly and nerdy. My eyes also took in the Nigerian major in his smart uniform, and the soldiers peering at me over the shoulders of the white men. Behind the group, my colleagues were gathered, the head of IT in the frontline, watching to learn why they had come to arrest Osaretin.

I nodded that I was me.

'Please come with us,' the man said.

The soldier took his hand off my shoulder and stretched it out to help me up. I looked at the ball, then immediately looked away, hoping I hadn't given it away. As I was being pulled to my feet I looked about for Rachel. She was standing next to Daniel, just outside the glass wall by the door. She looked steadily back at me. I ever so slightly turned my head and she, just as slightly so as to be unnoticed by anyone not in the know, nodded. She would get my ball.

Standing, facing the tall white man, I asked, 'Who are you? What is this about?'

'Come with us.'

I wanted to say no and stand my ground, but the soldiers, their guns, my colleagues busy-bodying, the madness of the past twenty-four hours, and of course the safe retrieval of my time-machine ball – the responsibility for which I'd delegated to Rachel, made going with them the only option. Also, it was quite apparent that no matter what I said, the tall white man's response was going to be 'Come with us,' so I left with them.

I think the entire population of the floor followed us as far as the door. The two white men stood on either side of me when we waited for the lift. I looked at Daniel standing by the door with the head of IT. The soldiers had pressed the button. A lift arrived behind us.

The two white men got in first and stood at the back of the lift. I stood in front of them, the soldiers stood in front of me, and their boss stood in front of them. The lift stopped on the third floor. The doors opened to a dozen or so executives, some of whom had taken impatient steps forward before stopping at the sight of the guns. On the ground floor the people waiting for the lift parted without being told and I was marched out of the building to a

95

waiting black Ford SUV. I was made to sit in the middle of the back seat, between the tall white man and the short, round one.

The driver was also white and also wearing a black suit. He had one of those curly white wires stretching from his collar to his right ear. He started driving as soon as the doors were closed.

'Where are you taking me? What is this about?' I asked.

I knew it had something to do with the night before. But because they had come with soldiers, I was confident they would not start talking about magic or claim to be magicians.

'Are you American?'

'Yes,' the tall man said without looking at me.

'Who are you?'

Silence.

'What did I do?'

The short man spoke. 'I'm Adrian, he's Richard, and he (he pointed at the driver) is Jason. Why don't you tell us about last night?'

I knew it. Where would I start? They probably knew about Adesua and Brother Moses. The two oddballs were probably, as they say, 'on their radar'.

Adrian didn't wait for me to answer. 'Yesterday, during the anomaly, all electrical devices with any sort of contact to the ground stopped working. Everything. Everywhere. Trains, computers, cars. The lot. They all

96

stopped working. Batteries became... strange. The electricity in them became... fuzzy, unstable, different. It's really quite... It's amazing. Contact with terra firma temporarily altered the nature of the electrical charge they stored. All through the event, not one single motor vehicle in any country in the entire world was functional, except two, and one of them belongs to you. How did you do it?'

'Do what?'

'Make your car work?'

'This is what this is about? My car?'

'We have your car. It's coming with us. Maybe you can help us understand why it wasn't affected by the anomaly.'

'Why are you calling it an anomaly? Didn't they say it was just a solar flare?'

'Right now, right this moment, trading has been stopped in all major markets. America is at DEFCON 1. Russia warmed up her silos hours ago. The world is one tweet away from global catastrophe. What happened yesterday was no solar flare. What happened was contact.'

'What?'

'Do you believe in aliens?'

I shook my head, glad I had not volunteered anything about Adesua and Brother Moses, but maybe they already had them too. Maybe the two were in the backs of similar black SUVs, between similar men in black, being questioned about the functioning of cars and being told about flying saucers.

'Yesterday was nothing short of an attack. They were

testing our defences. Your car could be the key to saving the world. Once we figure out why your car worked during the event, we'll know how to prepare when the first wave comes.'

'First wave?'

'That's right. They've probed. They've learnt our weakness. Now they will attack.'

'How can you be sure about all this?'

'How? 'Cus we've been dealing with them since Roswell. Heck, since way before Roswell.'

'UFOs are real?'

'They're real. And they're getting ready to attack.'

'So, where are you taking me?'

Before he could answer, the driver pressed the forefinger of his right hand to his earpiece. 'We've got a boogie,' he said, returning his hand to the steering wheel.

'Where?' Richard asked. Richard was the tall one.

'Nine o'clock.'

Adrian grabbed my arm. He looked even more excited than when he told me about an impending alien invasion. 'Have you ever seen a UFO?' he said. I shook my head.

'Well, take a look.'

He pressed a button to wind down the tinted window on his side.

He squinted at the brilliance of the sun and, shielding his eyes with his hand, began to search the sky.

'There,' he said, pointing. 'Do you see it?'

I leaned forward to see the UFO. At first I saw nothing,

then a tiny silvery dot moved from its stationary position and suddenly stopped again, as if to keep up with our fast moving vehicle. It was just a dot in the sky, reflecting the sun, but the way it moved and stopped was out of this world. I was looking at a real UFO. A real-real UFO.

Adrian reached behind me to receive something from Richard.

They were going to engage the UFO with some high-tech weaponry, and I was going to witness it.

Adrian collected the device and, holding it to his face, aimed it at the dot. I couldn't wait to see what it was. It was a camera. Was he taking pictures before blasting away at the aliens, or was the secret weapon disguised as a camera?

'They don't like being photographed, so when we see one of 'em watching us, we start taking pictures and they scamper real quick. Look, it's gone.'

The dot was gone but I hadn't seen it go and this filled me with such disappointment. I searched the sky but Adrian rolled the tinted window up.

'We've got a tail,' the driver said. 'Looks like… Looks like the other car.'

'What?' said Adrian.

He turned to look out of the rear window. So did Richard, and so did I. Adesua's car was right behind us. She was driving, and next to her, without his hat, was Brother Moses, smiling and waving at me.

Chapter 12

A Long Short Ride

There I was, being carted away, full of angst over Adesua's whereabouts and whether they'd found her too (unlike me, she and Brother Moses would have had a lot of explaining to do), and what does she do? She turns up behind us on Awolowo Road.

Straining my neck to look at her through the back window of our SUV, I realised I still liked her. No. I never stopped liking her. I felt it in my heart then in my belly. I really, really liked her. It didn't matter that Brother Moses had told me it was just a spell. The spell hadn't broken.

'She's nobody,' I said.

Adrian looked at me. 'You know her?'

I shouldn't have said anything.

'What should I do?' Jason said, looking in the rear-view mirror as he drove.

I saw Richard pull out a gun from his jacket.

'Stop the car.'

We slowly came to a stop. Adesua stopped a few metres behind us.

As Richard climbed out, Brother Moses also got out of Adesua's car. I moved to get out but Adrian held my arm.

'Hold your horses,' he said. 'Let the soldiers handle

this.'

'Soldiers?'

'Yeah. They'll bring 'em in.'

He looked out of the front window and only then did I realise that the white Hilux bus in front of our car was carrying the soldiers. They'd stopped too. I looked back.

Adesua stayed in the car. Her hands were on the steering wheel.

She stared at me, her face giving nothing away, yet in the blankness of her composure I could see that she was seething. At me. I should have followed her and Brother Moses before the men in black got involved.

What would she say when she found out I'd also lost the ball?

Richard's back came into view between the two cars. I could tell he was pointing his gun at Brother Moses. Adesua kept looking at me. Brother Moses, wearing his amazingly consistent smile, started juggling coloured balls that seemed to appear from nowhere. He moved to the front of Adesua's car and started hopping from one foot to the other as he juggled the balls, smiling.

'What the hell?' Adrian said.

I was also wondering what Brother Moses was doing.

'Alright, that's it,' Adrian said. He pressed down on the earpiece in his right ear. 'Let's get this clown, and the broad.'

The soldiers walked onto the scene, led by their boss. The major stopped by Richard, levelled his pistol to the

American's head and bang. Like slow motion, I watched the other side of the agent's head explode in a spray of red.

'What the!' Adrian screamed. He pulled out a pistol from under his jacket, dropped it in his lap and fumbled to hold it up again. 'Drive, drive, drive!' he said to Jason. The engine revved, the tyres screeched, but we did not move. What was going on?

The soldiers opened fire. Brother Moses pulled a long red umbrella that was way too long for his sleeve, out from his sleeve. He opened up the umbrella and, twirling it, deflected bullets from the soldier's guns. Adesua remained calm in the car. The four soldiers were perfectly lined up in front of the umbrella-twirling Brother Moses, using up their ammunition. They all ran out of bullets at the same time and, as one, they began reloading mechanically. Brother Moses peeped over the top of his now unmoving umbrella and I saw Adesua opening her door. What was she doing? She was going to get killed. Where was the major? Our tyres kept screeching. The car sort of zigzagged about for a few feet around its axis, as if we were tethered to the ground. Shots went off by Jason's door. He ducked. The shots left crush marks on his window but didn't make it into the cabin.

The engine died. Adrian was shouting into his sleeve – into a microphone, no doubt. There was terror in his eyes.

The major stopped to reload his pistol. Jason already had his out. I hoped he wouldn't do something foolish like open his door. Just as that thought was passing through my head, I heard the handle on my door being tried. I think I leaned into Adrian and held him. The major leaned towards the car and cupped his hand against my window to see in through the tinted glass. His face was disconcertingly blank. His men kept shooting. I couldn't see Adesua anywhere. A gunshot went off and plastered the major's exploded face against the window. His head slid down leaving a trail of blood. Adesua was standing there, smoke curling up from the barrel of the pistol she held in one hand. She turned sideways, to the rear of the SUV, aimed and shot. Bang, bang, bang, bang. I looked out of the rear window. The soldiers were slumped on the ground. Brother Moses closed his umbrella and inserted it back into his sleeve.

Adesua knocked on my window. She signalled for me to come out.

'Don't get out,' Adrian said, holding my arm. His hand was shaking.

'It's ok, I said. They're my friends.'

I unlocked the door. It was heavy. I pushed it open with my leg.

Adesua held her hand out for me. I stretched my hand to her and a gunshot went off close to my ear.

Adesua looked surprised. Still holding her hand out, she looked down at her chest. Her blouse was turning red from the middle of her breasts. She slowly fell backwards, her face still puzzled, her hand still stretched out to me.

Chapter 13

Faith the Size of a Ball

Jason had shot Adesua. She lay sprawled on the ground, her arms spread out on the road, the lifeless body of the possessed major at her feet. Jason had killed her. He had killed the woman I loved.

The entire world went weird. It was as if I was underwater. Sounds were distorted, voices were muffled. I was sinking where I stood. I was standing and suffocating.

I panicked. I swam towards the surface. I broke through and gulped in air tainted with gunsmoke and I screamed from the very depth of my heart, 'Adesua!'

Brother Moses walked up to Adesua's body. He shook his head and looked up into the car. His smile had turned upside down. I feared that Jason would shoot him too. I stepped out and Adrian followed me. I stepped over the dead major and stood by Brother Moses and looked down at Adesua. Adrian stood on the other side.

'You have to use the ball now,' Brother Moses said.

I immediately understood. Since they gave me the sphere I'd being alternating between fantasising that the unusually heavy tiny ball could really do what he said it could, and that it was just a ball of osmium that could do no more than surprise one with its weight. But now

I believed that it was indeed a time machine. I believed that magic was real. I believed that Brother Moses was a magician and that my father had been one too. I believed it all because I needed to believe that the magic in the ball could take me back in time to when I was in my flat and Adesua was still alive. I had to believe. I had to have faith in magic. I believed in magic. I put my faith in magic. I had to.

'I don't have it.'

'You lost it?'

'I know where it is. We have to get to my office.'

'What time is it?'

I checked the time. 'Three o'clock.' I double checked. 'That can't be.'

'Time is working against us. We have to hurry. The ball only works for twelve hours.'

'What?'

'It was precisely four o'clock this morning when I gave it to you. In one hour's time it will expire. We have to get to your office as soon as humanly possible.'

'We can get there in ten minutes.'

'You don't understand. They have co-opted time. Time is now working against you.'

I paused momentarily as I tried to understand what he'd just said before realising I didn't have time for that. I had to get back to the office. I had an hour. Adesua had an hour. But time was racing at an abnormal speed.

'I am going back to my office,' I said to Adrian.

106

He didn't object. He just nodded. Jason took his cue from Adrian and stayed at a respectable distance from my Adesua, whom he had killed.

All the shooting had emptied the road. Brother Moses and I put Adesua's body onto the back seat of her car. I climbed into the driver's seat, and Brother Moses slid into the passenger seat beside me. I made an illegal U-turn and pointed Adesua's car in the direction of my office. I checked the time. It was 3:15. How was that even possible? In the mirror I saw that the Americans were following us. I heard sirens. I couldn't tell where from. I pressed down on the accelerator.

'Did you see me mesmerising him?' Brother Moses said. His smile was back. I didn't understand what he meant.

'When I was juggling. I mesmerised him. The white man. A pity the soldiers were touched. No one had to die. No one.' He shook his head, his smile briefly going away.

I checked the time. 3:25. I'd only been driving a few seconds!

I didn't slow down at the roundabout. As I reached the street where my office building was I saw police vans racing towards us. I came to a screeching stop in front of the entrance and jumped out. I ran through the front door of the building, startling the doorman who had stepped out to tell me I couldn't park there. I ran to the lifts. I pressed the call button and waited in front of the lift that would arrive first. I punched six and for the first time noticed how slow the lifts were.

I pulled at the door of the IT floor, but it wouldn't open. In my panic I had forgotten to use my card. In slow motion, I took it from my pocket and held it to the scanner. When I finally got inside most of my mates had left. The ones who remained stared at me. They'd seen me being taken away earlier. They probably weren't expecting me to be back.

Rachel wasn't at her desk. I rushed to the meeting room. The glass had been cleared from the ground and the broken stool removed. My sphere was not there.

'Where is Rachel?' I said to no one in particular.

Some of my colleagues had got up to watch me. Some had moved out from behind their desks, but they were all keeping a safe distance, as if I'd become toxic. They just stared silently.

'Where is she?' I said much louder.

Amina, a cute girl who I had once asked out, answered with her sweet little voice, 'She left about an hour ago.'

I checked the time. 3:45. There was no way I could get to Rachel's house in fifteen normal minutes. But I had to try. I ran from the IT floor, not bothering with the lifts – I somehow knew they would take too long to arrive. I took the stairs, two steps at a time, jumping off the last three at each landing. I ran into the lobby and towards the exit and came to a sudden stop. Police cars surrounded Adesua's car, boxing it in against the front of the building. Policemen with guns aimed stood in front of their vans.

Brother Moses' head was visible above the roof on the far side of Adesua's car, coloured balls rising and falling in perfect rhythm over him. I checked the time. 3:53. I had to continue. I walked out through the front door. All eyes were on Brother Moses. I looked to the ground and went round the building to the car park. I had my car keys in my hands but my car was gone. I looked around and saw Rachel's red Camry, and she was in it.

I opened her door. Her key was in the ignition. Her seatbelt was fastened across her body but her hands were on her lap, one cupping the other. She looked at me. I couldn't tell whether she'd been crying or if it was something else. I didn't have time to ask.

'The ball, do you have it?' I said. I checked the time. 3:58.

She started to talk but her voice failed. She cleared her throat.

When she spoke, her voice was low and her speech so measured and so full of fear. She said. 'When they took you away, I realised it had to do with the ball. When no one was looking I took it. I knew it was important to you so I left the office in case they came back for it.'

'Where is it?'

'In my hand.'

'Can I have it? Please?'

A single teardrop fell down from her eye, then another from the other eye. Then more, but her face remained calm and she didn't move her hands.

'I can't,' she said. 'I can't move my hands.' She opened the fingers of her left hand which was rested into her right hand. The ball was buried in the middle of her palm, halfway through her hand.

I pushed my fingers around the sphere but it had become too heavy to lift. A tear from Rachel's eyes fell on to the back of my hand. 'What is happening?' she said.

'It's all going to be fine,' I said.

I'd just realised I knew how to use the sphere.

Chapter 14

Once Again One More Time

I did not know what to expect but I braced myself. Dizziness hit me like a gust of wind but I wasn't caught off guard as I'd been expecting worse, and I knew I just had to stay calm till it was over.

'I am leaving you my hat,' Brother Moses said.

We were in my living room. Adesua was also there, looking at me as if she despised me. But she was alive. I wanted to go and hug her but my head was still spinning and I had to stay in place or else I'd fall.

'No need. I'm coming with you,' I said.

'Oh. Well, that's wonderful. What a good choice you have made.' He picked up his hat and placed it on his head. 'I was afraid we would have to do this over and over again.'

I looked around. It still felt like waking up from a dream. My memory was only just catching up. I guess the brain is not designed to remember in reverse.

My tummy grumbled. I placed my hand over it. I could still taste the strange ball. The instant I placed my mouth over it on Rachel's palm I felt the sphere dissolving on my tongue, multiplying in volume a hundred times, spreading over every inch of my mouth and rapidly moving down the walls of my throat. At first I saw everything rapidly moving in reverse as if I was sitting backwards while being driven along the path I'd taken to get to Rachel's car. I moved faster and faster through time until the world was whizzing by and all the colours merged together into white, only to separate again as the rewinding slowed down and then stopped at my living room.

Adesua opened the door and kept it open. 'Let's go, then,' she said.

Brother Moses waited for me to go through first. As I passed him he said, 'One more thing, when you went to your room to jump, you said... I know. I shouldn't have said I was coming when I was leaving.'

Brother Moses stared at me from the doorframe.

'How did you know what I was going to say?' he said.

Up until that moment I thought we all knew what had happened since the last time we were all standing in my living room and he was giving me the ball to record time. It quickly dawned on me that only I had come back in time.

'He used the ball,' Adesua said.

'When did you use it?' Brother Moses said.

'Just now,' I replied. 'I mean, it was just before four o'clock. PM.'

'What made you use it?'

I looked at Adesua. Her face did not hide her contempt, and that was even without knowing that I'd gotten her killed.

'I was running out of time,' I said.

'Yes, yes. But what compelled you to use it?' Brother Moses said.

'Does it matter? We are here now and I am coming with you.'

Adesua stepped close to me. 'Listen. This is not a game. The only way you could have known you were running out of time is if one of us told you. The only way we'd have told you is if we were with you. The only reason we'd have been with you is if you were in danger. The only reason you'd have had to use the ball is if we couldn't save you. And the only reason we wouldn't have been able to save you is if we were dead. Who died? Both of us?'

I kept my mouth shut.

'Master Osaretin,' Brother Moses said, 'this is important. We have to know who died.'

'Why?'

'When a person dies, they slip into a place from where even time cannot escape. You can go back in time to warn them, but something is forever lost to that place.'

'What?'

'There is no way I can explain it that you would understand. Please, just tell me, who was it?'

I looked at Adesua.

'What!' she shouted. She threw her hands up and turned her back to me.

'How did it happen?' Brother Moses said. He was the most sombre I'd ever seen him.

Adesua marched up to me. She raised her fist to my face. She unfolded her index finger and pointed it at my forehead. She didn't let loose what she kept behind her gritted teeth. She breathed out slowly and dropped her hand like she'd given up on something, then she turned and began walking away down the corridor.

'What's going to happen to her?' I said.

'It depends on what you tell me. How did she die?'

'She was shot.'

'Who shot her? You?'

'No!' I was mortified. How could he even think that?

'Was it a person or something else?'

'It was a person. I think. An American. Secret service. He wore a black suit. There were three of them. They came to my office to get me.'

'Why?'

'They tracked down my car. And yours. Our cars were the only ones that worked during the solar flare.'

'I told her that was reckless.'

'So what does it mean for her? I mean, knowing the person who shot her, what does that mean for her?'

'Where was she shot?'

'In the...' My memory served up the image of Adesua lying dead on the ground. I couldn't say it. To voice it would be to make it real all over again. I pushed my finger into the middle of my chest.

'Mmm.'

'What's going to happen to her?'

'We shall have to wait and see. We have to go now. Remember, they know you are here and they are waiting for you downstairs. Adesua will distract them while I take you away.'

'Where are we going?'

'I told you already. To see a great magician. He will help you remember who you really are.'

Chapter 15

Soulful Penance

What Brother Moses told me was that basically I'd damaged Adesua in some irrevocable way.

Because I had not agreed, the first time they asked, to go with her and Brother Moses to meet the great magician, when my car had been tracked down to the office by the Americans I had been there, which resulted in my capture and, ultimately, in Adesua being shot. I killed her.

The immense, indescribable relief I felt when at 3:59 I felt the sphere working and experienced time rewinding gave way to the same sunken feeling I had when I watched her body lying lifeless on Awolowo Road.

She was alive again, but she was not complete, or the same, or Adesua anymore. I knew what Brother Moses didn't tell me. It was her soul that was missing. The part of a person which makes them human. The same part which cannot escape death.

Pain, horror, regret, shame, love, and sorrow flowed through my soul. At least I still had a soul. If there was a way I could give mine to her, I would. I, who before that day had not believed in souls, would give her mine. And it wouldn't be an act of penance; it would be for love. If only it were possible.

'You cannot give her your soul,' Brother Moses said.

'Did you just read my mind?' I asked.

We were at the entrance to my block, at the foot of the staircase, waiting for Adesua to lead them away.

'Yes, I did, Master Osaretin. You have to learn how to think quietly. It's one of the first things you'll be taught in your training.'

'Think quietly? How long have you been reading my mind?'

'Oh, just this one time. I didn't mean to, but you were thinking so loudly. It's a matter of etiquette that magicians don't try to read each other's minds.'

He peeped out of the open front door. 'We can go now.'

I followed him out of the building just in time to see Adesua's car being followed out of the compound by Rachel's car – only it wasn't really Rachel in the car. It was them.

'Keys?' Brother Moses said. He held out his hand.

I was about to remind him that the American agents had my car when I remembered that had happened in the future.

I gave him the keys. I could not imagine he'd ever driven a car before.

'Did you drive it down from the club?' I asked.

He shook his head. 'No. Adesua did that. Very reckless.'

'What? How? She drove her car here then returned to

118

get mine?'

'No. She drove both cars. At the same time.'

'How?'

'Ask her.'

He opened the driver's door and handed the key to Adesua sitting behind the wheel. I'd just seen her driving away in her car, and I was sure she wasn't there in mine a few seconds earlier when Brother Moses asked for my keys. Things just kept getting weirder and weirder.

Brother Moses sat next to Adesua in the front and I got in behind them. It was the first time I had ever been a passenger in the back of my own car.

Adesua was silent. She started the engine and pulled out. She didn't as much as cast an angry look at me in the mirror. If I couldn't give her my soul, what could I do?

'You can bring it back,' Brother Moses said.

'How?'

'By going where it is.'

'But you said nothing can escape death.'

'I know a great magician who once did.'

'Who?'

'Your father. And so can the son.'

'But he is dead.'

'Yes. But he once went into death and returned.'

'You mean he died and came back?'

'No. Think of death as another dimension. He discovered another way into this dimension and he went there.'

'Why?'

'No one knows. Maybe just because he could. He was a great magician, and so are you. You can do everything he could do.'

'But he is dead.'

'Yes. Now he is. But then he wasn't. No one knows how he did it, but once you start to believe in who you are, you too will be able to go into death and bring back that which has been lost.'

I looked at Adesua for a reaction. She drove in silence. Perhaps it wasn't really her. Perhaps the real Adesua was still leading them away and what was driving my car was a facsimile of her. A soulless avatar.

Soulless. The word rang through my mind. I was responsible for the loss of her soul. What was the effect of having no soul, anyway? I knew it must be infinitely terrible, but in what way and with what ramifications, I had no idea.

Adesua looked at Brother Moses.

'You really should learn to guard your thoughts,' Brother Moses said. 'It is rude to call someone soulless. What ramification? When she does die, her soul will have been dead for many years. She will then spend the rest of eternity as the person she was on the day she first died.

Whatever she does after that day, whatever joy she's had, whatever love she's known, all of these things, will be lost because her soul will not have experienced them.'

'Unless I bring it back. Unless you bring it back.'

Adesua turned round to look at me.

'Let's get one thing straight. I don't need you to save me or to save my soul. I knew this was a bad idea from the start. Five people are already dead. The last thing I want is for you to do something stupid and get yourself killed as well. Just stay away from me and my soul, and maybe no one else will get killed trying to save your foolish arse.'

It was Adesua in the car, alright. And she was as pissed as anyone would be if they'd been killed in the future due to someone else's mistake and their soul was lost through no fault of their own.

When Adesua was done she returned to driving, staring straight ahead. Brother Moses did not get involved.

I sat quietly and remorsefully on the back seat thinking of Alsatians, Suya, Afrobeat, UB40, Santa Claus, Albert Einstein, Moluwe, Herbert Macaulay, Dracula. Anything but how I was going to learn magic and go and get her soul back.

Chapter 16

A Sleight of Hand

Trying not to think of something is to continually think of that very thing.

I realised I needed to be distracted if I was to stop thinking so loudly that Brother Moses and, I now realised, Adesua as well, would not be able to read my mind. I looked out the window. I'd not been paying attention to where Adesua was taking us. I realised we were on a road in Lekki phase one. From the way she'd slowed down, it seemed she was going to turn into the new automatic car wash that just opened there. But surely my car was not that dirty, and even if it were, we were going to see a great magician as a matter of considerable and yet to be fully explained urgency, and we did not have time for this. Unless, of course, the great magician worked at the car wash?

She turned into the yard.

A car drove out the other end of the car wash machine and Adesua positioned my car to go in next. It made no sense. A tall, dark fellow who I'd tipped a few times came to the window and looked surprised to see who was driving. He looked in the back and his face broke into a smile.

'Bro, long time,' he said and extended his hand to me through Adesua's window, causing her to lean away to avoid him.

'Inside and outside?' the fellow asked. His name was Ali, according to his name badge which I'd never bothered to read before then.

'Top only,' Adesua said.

He said, 'Top to bottom?'

She said, 'Top to top.'

'Where?' he said.

'The glasshouse,' she said.

'Ok. Roll up all your windows and don't use the horn.'

He stood away from her window as she rolled it up and he waved us on with a yellow rag that had been hanging from his back pocket.

I was still trying to make sense of the conversation he and Adesua just had when she rolled slowly onto the conveyor. The yellow, blue and red rotating brushes got closer as we were drawn into the machine. The windshield became blurred under the spray of water and the frenzy of brushes. Inside the car became dark as we were completely enveloped.

Then, as we came out, the sun shone in brightly through the windshield and, in time, through the rest of the windows as we exited the wash. The vast open desert ahead of us looked too real to be an optical illusion or a painting on a wall. I turned to look at the car wash machine we'd just been through. There was nothing behind us except brown sand beneath and blue sky above.

'What's going on?' I said. 'What just happened?'

Adesua kept driving straight into the endless desert, kicking up sand in our wake. Brother Moses said, 'Relax, Master Osaretin. You're almost home now. Just relax.'

<hr />

I opened my eyes and did not know where I was. A few seconds later, I was sure, it would all come to me and it would be just like any other episode of waking up and not knowing where you are for a few confused moments before you realise where you are. I sat up on the white sheets and felt the bed wobble under me. I instinctively planted my hands and by so doing caused another gentle wave that slowly dissipated when I stopped moving. It was disconcerting. The sheets were white. The floor was white. The ceiling was white. The curtains were white. The curtains stretched from ceiling to floor all around. All white. I did not know where I was.

'Adesua! Brother Moses! Adesua! Brother Moses!'

The curtain fluttered in front of me. It parted at the bottom. A black cat walked in silently on its little paws. Its raised tail dragged the curtain with it as it sauntered into the room. It looked up at me with its yellow and black eyes and it continued round the unstable bed. It circumvented me, then once it had arrived back at the curtains where it had come in, it stopped mid-stride and turned its head to look at me. It winked, in the indecipherable way cats do, then it looked away, used its head to open a path through the curtain, and it was gone.

I leaned forward, the bed wobbled, and I whispered, 'Adesua. Brother Moses.'

The cat's head appeared through the curtains, its eyes on me. It took a step into the room, paused, paw raised and perfectly still. It took one more stride and stopped, then another, all the while looking at me. I got the feeling it was going to attack me.

'Adesua! Brother Moses!'

The cat turned and left the room again.

I was afraid to leave the bed. I was afraid of the black cat and the wobbly bed and the white room. I looked about. I couldn't see any source of light but the room was bright. What was beyond the curtains?

Where was I? Where were Brother Moses and Adesua? I was terrified.

The curtain fluttered. As if it had been pinched at two spots by invisible hands, it began to lift and part. I held my breath. The curtain stayed up by itself and Brother Moses walked in, smiling.

'Master Osaretin,' he said, 'everybody can hear you. Reginald said you didn't greet him.'

'Reginald? Who is Reginald?'

'He came in here to get you. You didn't say hello.'

'No one came in here. Oh. A cat. A cat came in here. Is that its name?'

'His name. He is one of the resident Grand Magicians

here, but I would advise you not to listen to him too much. He claims he has discovered a new dimension but his theories are suspect. He talks freely about his discovery of elastic time but he hasn't performed any tricks using his new dimension. He claims that dinosaurs are only as large as pigeons. He says that it is the expansion of time that stretches everything. All matter, he claims, will one day appear gigantic to other life forms to come. One day, he claims, our bones will be dug up by future humans and they will say we were giants. But he is a Grand Magician and you should have been more respectful to him.'

'A cat. It was a cat.'

'Reginald. Grand Magician of the First Order. If you will follow me, there are others waiting for you.'

'Where are we?'

'A place where magicians meet. Come. Let's go and meet the rest. They are all here for you. They are waiting for you.'

I tried to get off the bed without making it wobble. Brother Moses was by my side when I looked up. He offered me his hand. I took it and climbed out of the unstable bed. I looked back and couldn't see what the white mattress was lying upon. I looked under it. It had absolutely no support.

Brother Moses had passed through the curtain. I hurried after him, suddenly feeling uneasy to be alone with the floating bed.

I entered a wide white hall with a double height ceiling

and a vast glass wall that looked out onto rocky terrain and a cliff several metres away. On the other side of the cliff, far far away, mountains stood, their peaks stretching dizzyingly into the sky. Brother Moses was standing with his back to the glass wall in front of a group of men and women, all different races, all older than me, all dressed in elaborate outfits of various colours, with oversized lapels, glistening studs, and sequins. The black cat flexed its tail in front of them. They were all looking at me and smiling, like Brother Moses.

'Where is Adesua?' I said.

'She's not here,' Brother Moses said.

'Where is she?'

'She is not here. Look. The rest are arriving.'

He pointed out of the window. Everyone, including Reginald the cat, looked. Outside, beyond the cliff, hundreds of tiny luminescent dots were scattered across the blue sky. I walked to the huge glass pane. The figures grew larger. They got closer. They were people. Flying people. Their clothes flapped in their standing or sitting positions as they were carried by an invisible force. It was the most amazing sight I had ever seen. One by one the flying people landed on their feet and gracefully transitioned to normal pace walking. Double doors opened and they walked in, men, women, old, young, tall, short, white, black, every form of human. They all gathered together, talking to each other as if they were continuing conversations that had begun as they flew, and formed a close circle round me.

A plump Aborigine woman with the face of a child and grey hair that moved in slow motion about her head, as if it was being blown by the wind, was first to talk to me. She said, 'Are you the one? Show us something. Do magic.'

She looked keen and excited, as did all the other faces surrounding me. The crowd parted and a tall black man with a grey moustache and goatee, wearing a white suit with tails and a white top hat, and carrying a white cane with a silver knob, walked through and stood in front of me.

'Master Osaretin Osagiemwenagbon,' he said. 'Do you come today of you own free will?"

I did not know what to say. Brother Moses was suddenly by my side. He leaned and whispered into my ear, 'I do.'

I repeated, 'I do.'

'Were you coerced by anyone here today, or by others not now present but whom you, if the opportunity arose, could identify?'

Brother Moses whispered into my ear, loudly enough for everyone to hear, that I must say, 'No.'

I said, 'No.'

'And do you now wish to learn the secrets of magic as practiced by the magicians here today, and the magicians before them, and the magicians before the magicians before them, and so on and so on to the very end and beginning of time with no end and no beginning?'

'I do,' Brother Moses whispered.

'I do.'

'Observe.'

The man showed me both his bare palms. Holding the right hand up, he put his left hand into his jacket and produced a note of a currency I did not recognise. Using the thumb and index of both hands, while the other fingers remained flared for me to see, he folded the note several times till it was a square about one inch across.

He held the folded money between the thumb and index finger of his right hand and once again showed me his left palm. He folded the fingers of his left hand into a funnel and, holding the note up for me to see once again, he placed it into the hole he'd made in his left hand. He folded in the fingers of his right hand except for his index finger, which he used to push the folded money into the cavity of his left hand. He showed me his bare right hand then he waved it over his bunched left hand and, presenting the left hand to me, told me to blow.

Brother Moses whispered in my ear, 'Blow.' I blew onto the fist.

The man opened up his left palm and the money had vanished.

With the index finger of his empty left hand he directed my attention to his right hand, which he turned around. The folded note was wedged into the middle of his right palm.

'This is the first trick,' the man said. 'It is sleight of

hand. You shall now demonstrate it as proof of your proficiency and worthiness.' He unfolded the note, smoothened it and presented it to me.

Chapter 17

The Great Schism

How can I describe how I felt? I had learnt of magic and of great magicians. I had travelled back in time. I had watched men and women fly as if it were nothing. I had gone through a car wash in Lagos and come out the other side into a mountainous desert. I had learnt a great discovery, that normal life is a cat's wink away from the extraordinary. I was in the midst of great magicians and they were inviting me to become one of them.

I took the money from the magician in white and looked around at the eager faces watching me in anticipation. I wished Adesua was there, to see me pass my first test and be initiated into that to which she already belonged.

I refolded the note along the fold lines on it. I held it up between the fingers of my right hand and showed my fingers. My heart swelled with expectation and with fear for I didn't know if I could do the trick, but yet I believed I could.

Brother Moses placed his hands under mine from the side. He held my hands and guided my fingers. He formed my left hand into a receptacle and made me place the money into it with my right. He folded back the fingers of my right hand except for the index and we both pushed the money into the hole of my left hand. Then he straightened the fingers of my right hand, with the index still in the left, joined them together and covered my left fist with it. He pushed my right index through my left hand, pushing the money down and moving the joined fingers of my right hand down at the same time. The note, hidden from my audience, pushed through into my right fingers and he placed my thumb on it. He pulled my right hand down to my side, turned my fisted left hand to the magician in white and pulled my fingers open.

They all clapped. It was nothing but a trick and I had been helped to perform it, yet they all clapped and cheered as if I had done something great. Reginald the cat raised himself onto his hind legs and silently clapped with his black paws.

'Do you have any questions for me?' the magician said.

Brother Moses whispered in my ear, 'I do.'

I repeated the same, 'I do.'

'What is it?'

Brother Moses whispered, 'Who am I?'

I repeated, 'Who am I?'

The magician said, 'It is not for any being, now created or to be created, to tell you who you are. This great mystery is yours alone. Through the course of your training, you shall learn many things. Among these will be something that is yours alone. Guard it well when you discover it.

'Have you any other question for me?' Brother Moses whispered, 'Yes.'

'Yes.'

'What is it?'

Brother Moses whispered, 'What is your name?'

'What is your name?'

'I am Professor Ochuko. I am a very great magician of the highest level of all magicians.'

With that he shook my hand and the rest of the magicians clapped and cheered, stepping forward in turn to shake my hand and pat my back and embrace me into their sweet, flowery scents. I had become one of them. Now to learn some real magic; especially how to get Adesua's soul back.

When all of the rest had gathered into groups, chatting, drinking, and eating cake served on gold trays by Brother Moses and the resident Great and Grand Magicians, Professor Ochuko held my hand and led me away to a quiet corner where three white seats with conical bottoms surrounded a round white table in the middle, also balanced on the tip of its cone. I hesitated to sit, in case I upset the balance of the cone. I watched Professor Ochuko sit without causing his seat to move and I gently sat as well.

'You must have many questions,' he said. 'You may now ask freely all you wish to know.'

I wanted to get Adesua's soul back. I concentrated hard on this one thought and stared him in the face.

'Are you trying to tell me something?' he said.

Ok. That didn't work. 'How can I get someone's soul back?' I said.

'You are talking about Adesua. It's a tragic thing, what happened. But you must not blame yourself for it. Things happen. People die. Souls are lost. There are bigger challenges ahead of you and ahead of us all. You have to move on.'

'It's my fault.'

'Yes, it is. But it has happened. You have to let go. What will happen to her?'

'She will live and she will die, but her soul will have long been dead by then.'

'Brother Moses explained it to me. I'm not sure I really understand.'

'Imagine being the president of a country in your lifetime, and then when you die you have no memory of it. You spend the rest of eternity never knowing you once ruled a nation.'

'So she won't know what she becomes?'

'Much worse than that. Far, far worse. With time she would have perfected her soul, so that when she died, she would spend eternity in a good place. Right now, her soul is not where it should be.'

'Hell?'

'No. Far, far worse. It is truly tragic. But you should not let this bother you.'

'How can I get her back?'

'Her soul? You must go where it is, and you must be able to come back. It is impossible.'

'But my father did it.'

'Yes, he did. It wasn't impossible for him.'

'Can I learn to do it to?'

He stared at me for a long while, then looked down at his hands. He spread his fingers then turned his palms up.

'It is possible,' he said. 'Let us place this on the back-burner. Today is your day. We are all here for you. Ask me any other thing you wish to know.'

'Like what?'

If all the magic I ever learnt was how to get Adesua's soul back, my life would have been well spent.

'Anything,' he said. 'Anything at all, except the other matter.'

I thought for a while.

'What does "do not put your hand inside the finger" mean?'

'Brother Moses has warned you not to do that? You will learn the meaning in the dimension where it is possible to put your hand inside the finger. You must also stop looking at yourself in mirrors too often.'

'Why?'

'Many mirrors are not our friends. Some of them are with us, but not all of them. The problem is that you can never tell which ones are for us and which ones are against us, so it's better not to trust any of them. Except unused ones.'

I thought about it. How can a mirror be unused?

'Unused mirrors?'

He nodded. 'It is safe to assume that the rest belong to the other side.'

'What is the other side?'

'That is a very good question, Master Osaretin. We have been called many names over the ages. We have been gods, angels, demons, witches, wizards, tricksters and magicians.

'In the travels of your training you will encounter many beings, many great magicians, and many unknown and unknowable forces. You will also encounter the conspicuous absence of one entity. It is the question over the existence of this one magician that has led to the Great Schism among all the magicians.

'There are those who, emboldened by the knowledge of this absence and a further secret knowledge they claim to posses, seek to become The One. They lust to claim the name, even if its power is as unattainable as it is infinite. They spread news of a better world that they claim they will call into being, and they seduce the minds of the people with false doctrines, dangerous paradigms, and endless hope.

'Then there is us, we who see in the absence of this one being the very proof of its omnipotence.

'The war is between us and them. In truth, any notions of good and bad probably depend on which side of the Great Schism you choose to stand.

'Brother Moses has told you who you are. You are Mr Magic. That is your performance name. Your father told him who you are. You are a truly gifted magician. Your powers will one day surpass your father's. To those on the other side, this makes you a threat, because you can claim the prize for yourself, or you can wait till one of them makes such a claim and then you will work to surpass such a magician's powers. Either way, you are a threat to them. They want you for one reason only: to destroy you, and it could be the destruction of your body or of your soul. We are lucky Brother Moses found you first.'

'What if he's wrong?'

'Do you think he's wrong?'

I was pondering this question when the other magicians started laughing.

'Reginald is telling his jokes. Have you met him?'

'The black cat.'

'Yes.'

'Come, let us eat and drink with our fellow magicians.'

We went to join the rest of the magicians crowded round Reginald, who was walking half circles back and forth in the circle they'd formed around him. Frequently they would laugh, but I did not hear the cat say anything.

Brother Moses came to stand by my side.

'This is a beautiful place, is it not?' he said. Congratulations on making it here.'

It was a beautiful place, with its floating furniture, and its enormous hall, and its gigantic glass walls, and the out-of-this-world view, but Adesua wasn't there and her soul was in a bad place.

'Is Adesua coming? No.'

'Where is she?'

'Back where we came from.'

'Where exactly are we?'

'On Earth. Time is used as a camouflage, but we are on Earth. If that is what you mean.'

'I have to go back.'

'You don't have to, you know? Now that you are here, you can stay here. You don't have to go anywhere.'

Chapter 18

Passages

The sky gradually darkened outside until it had faded to deepest black, sprinkled with more stars than I'd ever seen. Together, the magicians all began to walk towards the wall of glass. The doors opened for them and they made their way into the night talking and laughing, holding hands or exchanging objects, until they gently lifted into the air and flew gracefully away, still having their conversations, still holding hands, still reading a pamphlet, or still waving at me as I watched them through the wall of glass.

I was filled with emotion as they were carried away, over the valley, growing smaller, taking on a luminous sparkle, until they were like fireflies spreading away across the sky, dissolving into the stars.

'Can you teach me how to fly?' I said.

Brother Moses was on my right. Professor Ochiko was on my left. It was he who answered me.

'Nobody has to teach you. It's like walking. First we learn to crawl, then we learn to walk, and if we keep learning, we fly.'

I was going to talk but he continued.

'You have many enemies. We can protect you from most of them, but you have a lot to learn if you are to defeat the strongest of them. Your training starts tomorrow. You are to begin at the bottom like everyone else. Remember to keep practising your coins.'

'Do you think I'm The One?'

He smiled. Without answering me he walked towards the doors and they swung open for him. He continued walking and then stepped into the air and floated away, brightening as he left, becoming a sparkling dot in the distance, and finally disappearing like a candle blown out far away.

'He doesn't think I am The One,' I said.

'Like I told you before, now that you are here, you are safe and you will always be safe here. You don't have to leave.'

'Why do you keep saying that?'

'You are safe here.'

'As opposed to where?'

'Anywhere else.'

'Like, home?'

'This is your home.'

'You know what I mean. Where is Adesua?'

'You won't be safe there.'

'But once I learn magic, I'll be safe there, right?'

'You don't understand. You cannot learn magic here. To learn, you must return. But you don't have to.'

'I want to.'

'Why? Because of Adesua? She does not need your help. She can look after herself.'

'Why don't you want me to go? Oh, I get it now. You don't think I'm The One. You made a mistake. You were wrong about what my father told you. That's it. I knew it. You are afraid I'll get killed because I will never be the magician you thought I was. When did you realise it? When are you going to tell the others?'

'I didn't make a mistake, Mr Magic.'

'I am not Mr Magic. If you haven't noticed, I am not special. I can predict lifts and coins, but those people, they can fly. Adesua, she can drive two cars at the same time, and you, you keep snakes in you hair. You know stuff. You brought me here. You gave me that ball. You know magic. If I can be taught magic, I want to learn it too.'

He sighed. 'You don't have to learn anything or do anything or be anything. I just want you to be safe and this is the safest place for you.'

'I can't stay here. Adesua is there and I need to learn how to get her soul back. Are you going to take me back or are you going to keep me here like a prisoner?'

'I cannot keep you here against your wish.'

'Good. So when do we go back? Now?'

'If you insist, we can leave in the morning.'

'Great. Where exactly are we going? Is there a school or something? Who's going to teach me? You?'

'We are travelling magicians. I already told you this. We go to places where people are not against the art of magic and we entertain them with our tricks. That is how we earn our living and this is where your training will begin.'

I vaguely remembered him calling himself a traveling magician and attempting to explain what that meant, but at the time I wasn't so keen on listening to what he had to say.

'What exactly do you mean by "travelling magicians"?'

'We travel from place to place and we put on shows for the people. What sort of places?'

'Places where they have never seen magic before. Villages. Small towns.'

'Doing what?'

'Showing them magic.'

'Why?'

'Because that is what we do. That is how we earn our pay.'

'Are you being serious right now? You want me to go from village to village performing tricks?'

'Not exactly what you expected, right? Remember, first we crawl, then we walk, then we fly.'

'You said something about people's imagination.'

'So you were listening. That is good. When you inspire awe through your magic, you unlock the minds of your audience. It's like opening a passage to another dimension. When it happens, you will know it. But first, you have to come up with a trick that is all your own. A trick nobody taught you.

Then, when you have performed it enough till it becomes like real magic to your audience, you'll see the doors unlocking. What happens then?'

'Then you walk into the passage.'

Chapter 19

Faka fiki

I woke up strapped down. I smelt petrol. In the time it took me to realise I was in the backseat of a Lagos yellow taxi, it also registered with me what portion of the Third Mainland Bridge we were on. In the same time, I noticed that Brother Moses had changed into normal clothes, namely a white shirt and no hat, and that the man next to him, driving as if he was running from the police, had a head all grey, and three, deep, lateral tribal marks etched into his fat, leathery cheeks. In the same space of time I became immensely angry.

'Why do you keep doing that?' I said.

Brother Moses looked at me. 'Ah, brother. You are awake.'

He winked and nodded at the driver and I realised that the elderly man was not one of us.

'Why did you do it?' I asked again.

The driver glanced at me in his mirror, then turned his head to look at me.

Brother Moses said, 'You must not talk too much. Remember, the doctor said you must rest.'

The driver had turned back to the road ahead, but his eyes still darted up to search my face in the mirror.

'I am fine. There's nothing wrong with me. Why did you do it again?'

'What did you do to him?' the taxi driver said.

Brother Moses laughed out loud like a bad actor. 'Don't mind my little brother,' he said. 'His medicine is making him feel funny.'

The driver looked at me in the mirror. He tried to make eye contact.

'Little brother, please, try to rest,' Brother Moses said.

'I am not your little brother. Why did you do it again? Why do you keep doing it?'

The car slowed down.

'What did you do to him?' the driver asked. He caught my eyes in the mirror. 'What did he do to you?'

Brother Moses laughed again and spoke quickly. 'My dear brother, I promise to make it up to you. You have my word.'

'Where are we going?' I said.

The driver slowed down even further. 'You don't know where you are going?'

'Home. We are going home.' Brother Moses said. He looked uncomfortable. I almost pitied him.

'And where would that be?' I said. I had him on the ropes.

'Faka fiki. To see our parents, remember?'

The words sounded like Yoruba, but Faka fiki was not among the little Yoruba I knew. I wasn't sure it was a place I wanted to go.

'Where is that?'

The driver stopped the car right in the middle lane of the Third Mainland Bridge, the murky water of Lagos Lagoon beneath us.

'What is going on?' he said, rather forcefully. 'Who are you people? Do you know this man? Is he your brother or not?'

'Yes,' I said. 'He is my brother.'

'Then why are you talking like he is kidnapping you?'

'I'm sorry. It's my medicine.'

'Your medicine? Are you ok now? Do you know where your family house is?'

'Yes. Faka fiki.'

'So why are you scaring me?'

'I'm sorry. Let's continue. We just need to stop at Ikoyi on the way.'

Brother Moses turned his head to look at me.

The night before, on the floating bed in the glasshouse on top of a mountain in the beautiful desert, I'd thought of the fear on Rachel's face when she had the ball in her palms, the magical journey back the next day, and learning to fly. I kept thinking of getting Adesua's soul back, and of performing magic for awestruck village kids, but my mind kept returning to Rachel. I had to see her and reassure her and apologise to her and let her know what was going on, using as many lies as it would take. I tossed and turned and caused the strange bed to wobble, but I couldn't shake the nagging feeling of a tap left running, a door unlocked, a stove left on under a forgotten pot of stew.

'I need to see Rachel,' I said.

'Don't you think it is safer to go straight home?' Brother Moses said.

'I have to see her before we go anywhere. Remember, you said you would make it up to me.'

'I just want you to think of your safety.'

The driver had still not moved. 'Where do you people want to go? Ikoyi or Faka fiki?'

Brother Moses sighed. 'We will stop at Ikoyi, then we will continue.'

We rode in silence to my office. We stopped on the other side of the road, and Brother Moses and I looked at my office building.

'What is your plan?' Brother Moses said.

I had none.

Brother Moses dug his hand into a duffel bag I didn't know he had between his legs and he brought out his hat.

'Wear this,' he said. 'Remember, the doctor said you must protect yourself from the sun.'

I took the hat and waited until I was out of sight of the driver before I wore it. If I remembered correctly, it had the ability to alter my appearance.

Facing the ground, I walked through the pedestrian gate. The guards didn't stop me. It was home time, and many of my colleagues and people from the other companies in the building would be leaving. I kept my face down and walked on to where I knew Rachel's car would be parked. Suddenly someone yelled out behind me, 'Osaretin.'

I froze. I imagined how stupid I looked with a purple hat on my head. I felt doubly stupid for thinking it would magically disguise me. I slowly turned round, ready to make a dash for it.

'Osaretin,' they called out again, and a child answered, 'Yes, dad.'

Little Osaretin in his school uniform skipped into the compound with two ice-lollies he'd bought from the ice cream van outside the building.

I did not have my pass, and even if I did, I could not just walk into the office and walk up to her. I would have to take off the hat so she would recognise me. I still remembered the episode with the men in black. It was too much of a risk. I went instead to her car and I was grateful when I saw that her windscreen was dusty. I checked that no one was watching then I wrote on it with my finger.

Chapter 20

Of Jasmine and Strangers

Rachel walked into the Jasmine Café. Her head was covered in a red scarf, which she had tied under her chin. Most of her face was behind a large pair of dark glasses, which were so dark I couldn't imagine she could see a thing through them in the dimly lit cafe.

I took a gamble when I scribbled 'Not your favourite flower' onto the dust on her windscreen. She had told me it wasn't, the day after she had a date there with a guy she tore to pieces when we talked about him in the office the next day.

Despite her scarf and oversized glasses, I could have picked her out of a football stadium full of Nigerian women. She walked over and sat next to me without looking up. I'd ordered two bottles of water and asked for a straw for her, as she would never allow her lips to touch the bottle. Watching her pursing her lips to suck, I realised why I'd needed to see her. I wanted her to be safe. I wanted to warn her not to talk to anyone about the ball, in case she spoke to the wrong person and they linked her to me.

'How are you? I said.

Without looking at me she whispered, 'fine.' She

sucked on the straw and peered over the rim of her glasses. There was a girl behind the bar scrolling through her mobile phone.

'I'm going away for a while,' I said. 'I don't know when I'll be back, but I'll keep in touch.'

'They are looking for you,' she whispered.

'Who is?'

'Everybody. They say you stole information.'

'What?'

'You hacked into the banking system during the solar flare. You and other members of Anonymous.'

'Rachel, I am not a hacker.'

'I know. Don't use my name.'

'I didn't hack into the banking system.'

'I know. They made you do it.'

'They? Who?'

'The 419 people who sent you that letter last week.'

'Last week?' It was just yesterday.

'Yes. They blackmailed you.'

'Rachel, no one blackmailed me.'

She pushed her glasses down the ridge of her nose to look at me. It hit me then. She didn't know anything from after I showed her the letter. The American agents, the ball growing heavy in her hand, that all happened in a future that had not happened again.

'Did you steal the data? Are you working with them?'

'No. No. I am not working with them. And I didn't steal any data.'

'So why have you not come to work since last week? Why are they looking for you?'

'Rachel, I… Look, it's a long story. But I didn't do anything wrong. You've got to believe me. I just wanted to make sure you are safe.'

'Safe? From what?'

'Nothing. Absolutely nothing. Did you tell anybody about the letter? Did anybody ask you anything?'

'No. What should I tell them if they ask me?'

'You don't know anything. And you haven't seen me since… last week.'

'Ok.'

She scanned the bar over the rim of her glasses, and she sipped her water from the straw. She quickly turned her face down to the table. I looked to see what she had seen.

A white man in a black suit had walked into the café and stopped at the bar. He leaned his elbow on the marble top. He was tall and slim. He had a full head of silvery hair slicked back, and a neatly trimmed moustache and beard. His face and arms were milky white. A gold watch glistened beneath the white cuff of his shirt. He caught sight of me, and his face brightened. 'As I live and breathe,' he said. 'It is you.'

I quickly looked down at the table, then slowly looked up again.

The man was still staring. He had a young face, despite his grey hair.

'It is him,' the man said to the lady behind the bar.

'You,' he said, pointing at me. He looked happy, like he'd found a friend from long ago. But something told me this was not a friend.

'Imagine finding you here. What are you doing? Hiding? Who's chasing?'

Chapter 21

The Plural of You

Sometimes you are so afraid you can't even move.

The strange white man with sleek grey hair and an immaculate beard walked to our table, undoing the single button on his jacket as he did. His belt buckle was a silver skull with tiny studs that sparkled as if they were lit from within. I noticed the tattoos on his fingers and on the back of his hand.

'May I?' he said.

He pulled out a chair and sat opposite me. Rachel was silent between us, looking down at the table. Perhaps she could also feel the terrifying force radiating from the strange man.

He placed his elbows on the table and clasped his long fingers together. He had tattoos of animals and insects between the joints of his fingers: a dog barking, a coiled snake striking, an eagle grabbing with its talons, a scorpion poised to sting. On the back of his left hand a swarm of bees flew out from his cuff. The hairy legs of a large tarantula spread across the back of his other hand.

He looked at Rachel's bowed head. He smiled and winked at me. 'She doesn't know, does she?' he said. 'Do you know who he is? Do you know who they say he is?'

'Who are you?' I asked him.

'How rude of me. I am Titus Titus.'

He unclasped his fingers and stretched his right hand across the table. He had tattoos on his palm too. The tips of the spider's legs curled around the edges of his hand, encircling many smaller spiders entwined in the middle of his palm. I hesitated. Knowing I shouldn't, but unable to stop myself, I shook his hand.

Something moved against my palm. I snatched my hand away. He clasped his fingers and looked me straight in the eyes. They were startlingly blue. The black in the middle was big. The blue looked deep and layered like a compressed picture of the universe. Looking into his eyes felt like looking down from the top of a tall, tall building.

'And you are Mr Magic,' he said. 'And this young lady here, what is your name?'

'Leave her out of it,' I said.

But it was too late. Rachel looked into his dizzying eyes and her body recoiled in slow motion. He offered her his hand. She kept her thumb back and only touched the tips of her other fingers to his. She snatched her hand back. She too had felt it.

'What do you want?' I said.

'The question is not what I want. I want nothing. But you, you want something and I can give it to you.'

'I don't want anything from you.'

'Oh, but you do. You want to know who you really are. You want to know who your father was. You want to know why everyone is looking for you. You also want to know what they really want from you. But most of all, you want to know why.'

'Why what?'

'Why. That's the one question boring deep into your being. You know that you don't know, but you don't know what it is that you don't know. And nobody is telling you. Why. It's eating you up. It's munching at your brain. You feel it. Munch, munch, munch.'

I grabbed my head in both hands. The throbbing stopped as suddenly as it had started.

'What are you doing to me?' I said.

Rachel was perfectly still, hunched into me. Her face was focused on him and frozen in place with fear. Where was Brother Moses? Surely he would have seen this man entering the café.

Titus Titus placed the tips of his fingers on the table and leaned forward. Rachel's body pressed harder against mine.

'You ask me who I am. You and I are the same. They call us magicians. Don't you just hate that word? I would rather they called me by my real name, wouldn't you? Have you shown her some of your tricks? Your rabbits in a hat? Your disappearing cards?

'Surely, we are more than that. We are more than what they call us. We are gods, and they are lost. We are more than superior. We are amazing, you and I. Awesome.

'You, woman, are you afraid of me? You should be.

Did your heart not start beating faster the moment you saw me? Did your sweat glands not go to work when I walked in? Those are the cells of your body reacting to superiority. Your body knows it. Your soul knows it. I am you, multiplied by infinity. I am incomprehensible to you. And you fear me for it. They all do.'

He looked at me. It felt as though thumbs were pressing my eyes into their sockets.

'You have been told to be afraid of things that go bump in the night. That's good. But you must also be afraid of things that go bump in the daytime too.'

He leaned forward. Rachel and I leaned further away, as far as we could go without tipping over. His grin flattened with a paralysing lack of emotion. He suddenly yelled, 'Boo!'

Rachel and I screamed. We jerked away from him, losing our balance, and I had to grab the table to stop us from falling.

Titus Titus tilted his head backwards and laughed. He stood up and buttoned his jacket.

'Do you know who he is? His new friends would have us believe he is the sum of all things. The recurring number. The solution to every equation. An irreducible quantity. They've been filling his head with all sorts of flattery. They're calling him the Mac Daddy. The real deal. The bomb. The shizzle. They say he's the cat's pyjamas. The real McCoy. The midnight cowboy. Or, like the English say, the dog's bollocks.'

He bent over and placed the tips of his fingers on the table. His grin gave way to a straight face. The black of his eyes grew to twice its size.

'They say you are magic personified, yet here you are, hiding amongst the humans you're meant to save. People don't want another prophet, brother. They need leaders.'

He stood up straight. He shook his head at me. 'You. Mr Magic? Not in a billion galaxies.'

He turned and walked away, out of the Jasmine Café.

162

Chapter 22

Things Missing

Rachel and I remained huddled together. Her arms were tightly wrapped around my body and she shook continuously. The barmaid walked back into the Jasmine Café. She stopped and looked at us as if there was something wrong with us, then she continued to the back of the counter where she looked at us again, a confused expression on her face.

'Is he gone?' I asked her.

'Who?'

'The man who was just here. The white man.'

'A white man?'

'Yes. He spoke to you. He just left. Is he still outside?'

'A white man? I didn't see any white man.'

'He talked to you. He just left. Did you see anyone outside?'

'Leaving this place? No.'

Rachel whispered into my ear, 'Osaretin, what is happening?' I tried to stand up but Rachel's hands held me back.

'He was wearing a black suit. He had white hair and a beard.'

The lady shook her head.

'Maybe it wasn't you. Where is the girl that was here when we came?'

'I am the only one here. I was here when you came. You arrived first, then she joined you. No other customer has come after you.'

Brother Moses walked into the café. From the look on his face I knew he knew what had happened.

'Has he left?' I asked him.

'Who?'

'The man. Titus Titus. Do you know him? Did you see him?'

'Titus Titus was here?'

'Yes. Didn't you see him? He just left.'

'No. I came in to see what was taking you so long. Where are your shoes?'

'What?'

I looked down at my feet. They were bare. No shoes, no socks.

Rachel as well. When she looked down, she curled her toes, she screamed, and she drew her legs onto the chair.

'Osaretin, what is going on?' she said, shivering in my arms, tears rolling down her cheeks.

'We have to go now,' Brother Moses said. 'Right now.'

'What happened to our shoes?'

'There's no time to explain. We have to go now.'

It was the first time I saw him afraid.

'I can't leave her here,' I said. 'She's coming with us.'

Rachel's grip tightened. 'Who is he?' she said. 'I don't

want to go anywhere. What is going on?'

Brother Moses answered her, 'He can't explain what just happened, but I can. We don't have time right now, though. If you want to live, you have to come with me now.'

Outside, even though the sun had begun to sink below the horizon, the sandy interlocking concrete slabs were warm beneath my bare feet. It took a few seconds for it to register that it was our taxi driving out of the compound. I shouted and raised my hand to wave the driver down. It was no use. Rachel held on to me tightly.

'We have to use your car,' Brother Moses said to Rachel. To me he said, 'Can you drive?'

I nodded that I could.

While Rachel, with trembling hands, searched her handbag for her car keys, I tried to make sense of my missing shoes. I didn't remember taking them off, or having them taken off. And, whatever had happened to take them away had happened to Rachel too. I felt terribly bad that I had exposed her to all this. But what had happened to our shoes?

'They took you.' Brother Moses said.

'What?'

'You've heard of alien abductions? You were abducted.'

'By aliens?'

'You can call them that, yes.'

'Why?'

'They wanted to know if you are the one.'

'Titus Titus is an alien?'

'You can call him that.'

'He said I wasn't Mr Magic.'

'Do you believe him?'

'How did they take us? We were in there all the time.'

'No, you weren't. If you saw Titus Titus, you were either on his ship, or on the moon. I doubt he took you to the moon. It would have been too risky for him.'

'I don't understand.'

'I don't expect you to. Titus Titus is the leader of the others. He has been looking for you for a long time. Now he has found you.'

'But why did he let us go?'

'I'm not sure.'

'Because I am not Mr Magic?'

'No. It must be something else. He's up to something. He has a plan.'

'Why did he take our shoes?'

'He makes everyone take off their shoes before they get onto his ship. He's got a thing about germs.'

Chapter 23

Fear and Serendipity

The little town of Faka fiki is unlike any I'd ever been to before. For one, at the end of the long, narrow, untarred road cut out of the forest that led to it, there was a wooden notice board that warned 'All male youth coppers' to 'keep your hands away from our daughters'.

The letters were written in white paint that seemed very white and clean against the old, decaying, dusty board. The warning was either recently done, or the community felt the need to keep the message fresh.

The undulating road was cocooned between the formidable roots of great Iroko trees on either side, which would not allow more than the slowest of progress. A few metres further along we came across yet another such noticeboard, this time warning 'Pastors, evangelists, men of God, turn back now'.

It was night already, but the denseness of the foliage, above which the cloud-covered sky stretched like a blanket of blackness, made the night even darker and caused the beams of the car's headlamps to feel like a careless announcement of our intrusion. I stopped when the beams lit up a third sign. This one made me want to engage the reverse gear. It was a wooden board as well, but this time

the letters were formed from shells. Just three letters.
S.O.S.

The engine purred into the night and insects danced
in the beams shooting from the bonnet. A gecko's eyes
glistened on the wooden board, then the reptile walked its
hypnotic walk across the letter O, climbed onto the top of
the board and lay flat on its belly, its eye fixed on us.

Rachel sat in the middle of the back seat and leaned
forward to look out through the windshield.

'I don't see any houses,' she said. 'I don't see anything.
What is this place? Where are you taking me? What are
you planning to do with me?'

I could hear the fear and panic in her voice. It broke
my heart.

'You will be safe here,' Brother Moses said.

'Osaretin, why are you doing this to me? Where are
you taking me? Osaretin?'

I understood her fear. I would be afraid too, if I
were her. And I was afraid, but for different reasons. She
thought she was being kidnapped. It wouldn't be the first
time a person got kidnapped in Lagos for the sake of so-
called money rituals. But after all she'd been through, all
she'd seen, ending with the encounter with Titus Titus, I
expected that she was fully in the know. Then it occurred
to me that I was still mistakenly thinking she experienced
the time machine ball that got too heavy to be lifted from
her palm – but that was in a different future. She really
didn't know much at all.

'Rachel,' I said, trying to sound calm even though I was just as apprehensive as she was, 'that man at the Jasmine café is a very bad man and we must hide from him.'

'What has it got to do with me?' she said, her voice sharp and challenging. Her brain had chosen fight over flight.

She looked me straight in the eye, unblinking and ready for the fight. It was as if she had been in a trance all along, all through the encounter with Titus Titus, all through the long journey through Lagos to the outskirts of town and finally onto the road to this mysterious town, and she had only just woken up to the perilousness of her situation. To be fair, it had been a little hazy in my head as well, ever since I discovered my missing shoes.

Brother Moses turned in his chair to look at her. 'It had nothing to do with you until Titus Titus saw you with him. Now he knows who you are and he will use you to get to him.'

'How?'

'Master Osaretin is a very special person. He has an amazing gift.

That is why Titus Titus couldn't hurt him. But now, Titus Titus has discovered a weakness. He is going to use Master Osaretin's love for you against him. That is why you must be protected.'

'Love for me?'

'Yes. You are like the sister he never had. He will do anything to protect you, and his enemy knows it too.'

Rachel looked at me. I was as surprised by his words as she was, but it made perfect sense. She was my best friend, we spent more time in fake meetings with each other at work than we did working, we watched out for each other, we waited to see new movies with each other, we trusted one another with our secrets, we took our problems to each other, and like me, she was also an only child. Why hadn't I seen it before now? We were both each other's only siblings. And with that realisation came the panicked thought that I had exposed her to immense danger and I had to protect her no matter the cost. And I just knew that the cost would be high.

Chapter 24

Late Night Hospitality

Rachel suddenly screamed and my heart leapt into my throat. Out of the darkness a short figure walked towards us in the beam of the headlights. He stopped and stood perfectly still. He was a frail old man, about four feet tall. He had a white cloth wrapped around his body and slung over his shoulder. He held a long walking stick that was taller than him by a foot and upon which he leaned his weight. The stick was stout and rounded at the top. Another man stepped out of the shadows into the light and stood beside him. They were the same height. Then another, then another, until there were about a dozen of them, short men, wrapped in white, holding sticks, which in the hands of the younger ones appeared to be weapons.

'Who are they?' I said. My heart was still beating hard and fast. I'd been deep in thought over Rachael's safety when she suddenly screamed.

'They are from the town. Let's go out and greet them,' Brother Moses said.

'Do you know them?'

'No. But they have come to welcome us, so it would be rude to remain in the car.'

He opened his door, stepped out, and left the door

open. He walked up to the men and started talking to them. It appeared he was talking mostly to the old man who had first stepped onto the road. The other men kept peering past them to try and see beyond the beam of the headlights into the car. They were all short, but they had sticks, and they outnumbered us considerably.

Brother Moses gesticulated as he spoke. He waved his hand at me, beckoning me to join him. Rachel grabbed my arm from behind. Her fingers seized a considerable chunk of my flesh but she needn't have worried; I had no plans to leave the car.

Brother Moses turned to look at me. He frantically waved for me to join him.

'Please don't leave me alone,' Rachel said.

'Never,' I said. Truth be told, I was too scared to leave the car.

Walking backwards, his steps matched by forward steps by the men, Brother Moses came to my window.

'Please, come out,' he said through his teeth as he maintained a smile for the men who were very close to the car now.

Rachel's grip tightened on my arm, but I'd realised I had to get out, if only to draw them away from her.

'I have to go,' I said.

We looked at each other. She didn't say anything. I opened my door and placed my foot out onto the strange land. She let go of her grip on my arm and opened her door as well. Before I could warn her to stay in the car, she was standing outside, waiting for me

I stepped out of the car. With both her hands, Rachel held onto my right arm.

'I present to you, Mr Magic,' Brother Moses said, holding his hand out at me. 'The greatest magician in Lagos, Ogun, and Ijebu. In fact, all of the Western Region.'

He paused, perhaps for applause that did not come. The men stood silently, their fingers wrapped around the stems of their cudgels.

The old man spoke. 'Your assistant said that the State Government has paid for you to perform magic shows for us. We need teachers, not magicians. Are you going to teach our children how to do magic shows like you so that they can go into the city and earn money?'

Brother Moses answered for me. 'Master Osaretin paid a lot of money to go to magic college in London. He cannot just teach you his tricks without some sort of payment.'

'But you said the State Government has paid for him,' the old man said.

'No, no, no, no, no, no.' Brother Moses shook his head and waved his finger. 'The government only paid for us to entertain you. They didn't pay for us to teach you the secrets of our profession.'

'What use is your magic show for us then?'

'If you don't want us to entertain your children with London magic like we entertain the children in Lagos, we are happy to leave right now. You just have to sign a document saying that we came here and you said you didn't want us.'

The men huddled around the old man and spoke in hushed voices. Like petals opening from a flower, the men peeled away from the old man and he spoke. 'We are not turning you away. You can stay and perform your magic show for the children, but when you leave, tell the government people that next time they should send teachers. And real teachers, not the youth copper ones.'

We drove slowly behind the men. They led us into their town, which was no more than a handful of unpainted bungalows with thatched roofs. I wondered why the houses were normal size with doors tall enough for someone my height.

Rachel continued to hold me tight as the old man showed us into the house we would stay in. The other men followed behind.

The town had no electricity and, from the looks of things, no running water either. Our 'guest house' was a bungalow that comprised a single corridor separating two rooms that had curtains for doors.

'Is he your husband?' the old man asked Rachel.

She shook her head.

'She will sleep here,' he said. He pulled back the curtain over the room on the right and held his clay lantern up. We all looked in. There was a mattress on the floor, on top of a straw mat the like of which I hadn't seen since I was a child. The room was bare except for the mattress.

'The toilet is out there,' the old man said. He pointed to a door at the end of the corridor. The toilet was outside? In the dark?

'You and you, you will sleep here,' he said. He waved his lamp at the adjacent room, leaving a trailing waft of black smoke.

'Thank you for your generosity,' Brother Moses said. 'I will make a note in my report to the State Government.'

The old man waved the kind offer away with his free hand. He stepped aside to allow the other men to exit the bungalow, then he stopped at the door and pointed upwards. I had not noticed the hole in the thatched roof until then.

'That is where the last youth copper who dared to lay his hands on one of our daughters was taken,' he said.

He made eye contact with me, then he passed under the hole, leaving me baffled by his cryptic, ominous piece of information.

Chapter 25

The Magician's Assistant

Brother Moses, Rachel, and I stood under the hole in the thatched roof and peered through it at the dark sky above. The hole was about a metre wide, maybe less, but enough for a person to have been dragged out through it. The disturbed fibres of the thatched roof were curled upwards at the edges of the near perfectly round hole.

'What does he mean, 'that was where a youth copper was taken'?' I said.

Brother Moses in his jovial voice explained. 'They are superstitious people in this town. They believe in spirits and ghosts and witches and wizards. They think something from above took a youth copper away through the hole.'

'Superstitious? There is a hole. Who made it? Where did the copper go?'

In my service year I was posted to a town in the North, not dissimilar to Faka fiki in its wide variance from everything I was used to. In that village in Gombe they also had their own gang of spirits that they entertained us with. But their own gods and spirits only demonstrated their amazing powers in the legends of the villagers; they did not leave gaping holes behind where they had

177

snatched youth coppers out through thatched roofs.

Brother Moses shifted and tilted his head as if to inspect the hole from another perspective.

'It may be that the youth copper was mischievous. He was warned not to touch any of the village girls or else a spirit would come and carry him away, so he made the hole to spook the villagers. They are very superstitious people, these people. You will see. Tomorrow, they will believe all of our tricks.'

'Superstitious? Tricks? Really? Really?'

'Yes, yes. They are really very superstitious. They have gods that they worship for almost everything. You will see. They are very backward indeed.'

'After everything that has happened, you are saying something could not have taken the youth copper out through this hole?'

'No, no. All I am saying is that it is a story the villagers tell to make sure young attractive men like you keep their hands off their daughters. Ah! I know. Maybe they made the hole themselves.'

'Why exactly have we come to this place of all places?'

'Because they are gullible. You would be able to easily mesmerise them with your tricks.'

'My tricks? I don't know any.'

'Do you have a coin? Show her your coin trick.'

'What is he talking about?' Rachel said.

I was keen not to get her any more apprehensive than she already was. While thinking of how to answer her, my mind replayed my ability to accurately call the face, and how I intentionally got it wrong each time Daniel tossed his coin, and suddenly it hit me; that was in the future that I came back from. There was no way Brother Moses could know about that.

'How do you know about the coins?' I asked.

'How do you mean, how do I know?'

'How do you know about my coin trick?' It felt deceptive calling it a trick.

'You can predict which way the coin will fall, can't you?'

'Yes, I can. But how do you know that?'

'Everybody knows.'

'Who is everybody? How do you know?'

'We all know. Remember, Professor Ochiko told you to keep practising your coins? Have you been practising?'

Perhaps there was nothing to my building suspicion.

'I don't have a coin.'

He put his hand in his pocket. I knew he could keep uncountable things in the tiniest of places. I quickly took Rachel's hand and led her to the room that had been designated as hers.

'I'll stay with you,' I said.

'That might not be a good idea,' Brother Moses said.

Rachel stopped, so I had to stop as well.

'I am only your manager. Your assistant will soon join us. What are you talking about?'

'You are Mr Magic, the magician from Lagos. I am

your manager, promoter, call me what you may, but every respectable magician has an assistant. Yours is joining us tonight.'

'Who is it?'

He simply looked at me as if I he expected me to know. I realised I did know. Adesua was coming.

Chapter 26

An App for Everything

Brother Moses and I sat on the doorstep in front of the bungalow to wait for Adesua. I felt he wanted to talk but I maintained a frown of deep thought, and sat facing slightly away from him so that he would not bother me.

What a fantastically dark night it was. Our neighbours' huts, metres away, stood in gloomy silence like painted shadows on an infinite black canvas. No lanterns shone through their windows. I'd heard no sounds coming from them. The nocturnal beasts made their night noises in the forest, whose borders were indistinguishable and shifting. The air was stiff and laden with the raw scents of vegetation, and the sky was an endless expanse of featureless blackness. Altogether, it was grim.

And it was hot. My palms were clammy, my armpits were moist, my entire body dreamed of a cold shower in a clean modern bathroom.

The rumbling noise of an engine grew in the distance. We saw the lights of the big noisy truck before it navigated the bend and pulled up in front of us. By then, Brother Moses and I were on our feet. It was a big truck. The driver turned off the headlights and killed the engine. Both doors opened. Adesua climbed out from the driver's side while a man, one of the villagers, hopped out of the passenger side. He didn't have a stick.

They joined each other in front of the truck and continued with a conversation they must have been having in the cab. As they walked up to us, Adesua looked at me ever so briefly, but the smile on her face was for the man she was talking to. The short chap was gesticulating with his hands, his little fingers flying all over the place like he was smearing invisible paint over an invisible wall. They stopped in front of us. Adesua placed her hand onto his shoulder, threw her head back, and laughed at whatever it was that he had just said. Before she recovered, he was telling another joke. I didn't care to try to hear it. I was sure it wasn't that funny. Adesua was only laughing to humour him. It was all part of the act to charm the natives.

'How did you do that?' Brother Moses said to me.

'Do what?' I asked.

'I can't hear your thoughts. How did you learn to block them?'

I did not know I was blocking him out of my head. In fact, had I thought about it I would have started thinking of Bruce Lee or Pink Floyd, or mentally doing the multiplication tables, because I was probably thinking way too loud, and of thoughts and notions I'd rather he didn't hear.

'I didn't do anything.'

He wasn't exactly smiling, but the way he looked at me, his face looked happy.

'It comes naturally to you,' he said.

Pride. That was what was on his face. He nodded slowly. He stared at me for a few moments longer, then said, 'Mr Magic,' and slowly nodded again.

Somehow, Adesua and her new friend had gone from standing next to each other to holding hands. They looked like a young mother holding the hand of her child, only the child was a grown man who was keen on making her laugh. He liked her, and he was trying to impress her with his jokes. I imagined all the jokes started, 'A tall man and a short man walked into a bar.' That made me smile.

Adesua and the man stood in front of Brother Moses and me, a smile still lingering from her laughter, and she introduced her new friend to us.

'Guys, this is Odedina. He's a hunter and a wrestler.'

The man thrust his hand up to me with much more swag than could possibly reside in such a small body.

I shook his hand. It was like having a child's hand in mine.

'What is your name?' he asked when I failed to introduce myself.

Had he not been in the welcome party? They all looked the same.

'This is Mr Magic,' Brother Moses said.

'You are the magician. Can you show me a magic trick?'

I wished I could show him how to make a man disappear.

'You have to come to his performance tomorrow to see that,' Brother Moses said. 'You will be mesmerised beyond your imagination. Tell everybody to come and see the show. It's not just for the children. Everyone must come. Tell them.'

Odedina swung his hand to Brother Moses. 'And you are?'

'His manager,' Brother Moses said, shaking the man's hand. 'Will you come to the show tomorrow?'

Odedina looked up at Adesua. 'As long as this lovely lady is there, I will be there.'

Adesua and Odedina laughed. It was precisely that. A joke. There was no way on Earth he had a chance with her. I hoped.

'I have to get some rest before tomorrow,' Adesua said, 'so I'm afraid I'll have to say goodnight now, dear.'

She bent to hug him and offer the sides of her face for him to kiss. His hands barely reached her shoulders. As he left, he stopped to wave one more time. Adesua waved back and he blew her a kiss. She caught it in her hand and plastered it onto her left breast. It was the most cringe-worthy thing to witness. And then he was gone, wobbling along into the night, his white wrapper the only visible thing as he disappeared into the distance.

Adesua turned swiftly to Brother Moses.

'Where is she?'

'Inside.'

Adesua stepped between us and went into the house.

'How did she know?' I said.

'It is her job to know everything. Her job is to protect you.'

'Yeah, yeah, but how did she know about Rachel?'

'I told her.'

'Telepathically?'

'No. I sent her a message.'

'How? When?'

'With this phone.' He pulled a smartphone from his pocket. 'I sent her a text message while you were driving. I'm sorry. Did you want to tell her yourself?'

'You have a phone?'

'Yes, yes. I must show you the apps I have on it. Remind me tomorrow. I just downloaded an app that makes things invisible. It's extraordinary. I have one that I made, it tells the precise weight of anything you photograph. Isn't that amazing? I made that one. It has been downloaded fifty-five times. It's not that popular yet. I think it's the name. I didn't come up with a good name. That's what is lacking; a good catchy name.'

'You built an app?'

'Yes, yes. Would you like to download it? I call it, "What does it weigh?" Not catchy, right? I know, I know. That's why it's not popular.'

'You built an app?'

'Yes, yes. Most magicians create apps. Maybe you will create some yourself. When you learn a new trick that only you can perform, before everyone else learns how to do it, you create an app for it and sell it to other magicians.'

There were so many questions, but talking to him about magician's apps only managed to temporarily distract me from what had led to the talk of apps in the first place.

Throughout the rest of the night I sat on the mattress on the floor in our room and watched the silhouettes of Adesua and Rachel through the curtain over their door. They were sitting facing each other on the mattress. A lantern burned between them. Adesua talked and Rachel sat still and listened.

Chapter 27

Stir Me Hot

Gunshots woke me up. From the sound of it, many guns were being fired by many shooters. I rolled off the bed, instinctively trying to take shelter under it, but I rolled straight off the mattress and onto the floor. In my panic, I had forgotten there was no bed to shelter under. Other than the mattress the room was bare, and there was no place to hide.

Brother Moses was gone. With my belly flat on the ground I looked through to the adjacent room. The curtain had been drawn back. The room was empty. The shooting stopped. There was something odd about it. A second later I began to laugh.

I got up and saw the clothes laid out on the other side of the mattress: a black suit, a black tie, and a white shirt. On the floor, a pair of shiny black shoes had been placed beside my trainers, next to my folded up clothes. Neatly rolled up silvery socks were sticking out of the new shoes. The fireworks started again. I knew the costume was mine, or rather, Mr Magic's, but it didn't feel quite right wearing such immaculate clothes before I'd taken a bath.

Had Adesua had a bath? Where? What about Rachel? Did she have new clothes too? I lifted the edge of the curtain over the window. Brother Moses was in his purple outfit, complete with his hat, standing amidst kids in front of the lorry. He was the one responsible for the fireworks, which were materialising ready lit from his wrists before he tossed them into the air to fully discharge their noisy essence, much to the delight of the cheering village children. I couldn't see Adesua or Rachel. I was keen to know what Adesua had been telling Rachel last night.

'Do you take hot or cold showers?'

I dropped the curtain as if I'd been caught doing something bad.

Adesua looked resplendent in her costume: black tights, shiny black boots up to her knees, a white shirt under a fitted black coat with a short tail, and a fluffy black scarf loosely tied round her neck. She also had a black top hat. We would look similar on stage. My heart skipped a beat. I was expected to go out there and do magic, and it wouldn't be like during my initiation when Brother Moses guided my arms. I would be alone and I didn't know any magic.

'Hot or cold?' she asked again. 'Warm.'

'Follow me.'

I followed her. I peered into the other room on our way out. It truly was empty. Adesua led me round the bungalow. The children were too caught up with Brother Moses' fireworks to notice us. Behind the bungalow there was a cubicle made of corrugated iron sheets set upon a concrete slab four feet by four feet. There was no roof over the shower stall. A transparent shower curtain hung over its one open side. She drew the curtain aside and held it up for me to step inside. There was a pail of water on the wet floor. A dry towel hung from a nail in a corner. It smelt of soap in there.

The curtain rested on her back as she bent to put her finger into the water. She stirred and removed her finger.

'Is that ok?' she said.

I put my hand into the water. 'It's ok, I guess,' I said.

'Not warm enough?'

'It's fine.'

'Is it warm enough or not?'

'I usually use very warm water. Almost hot, in fact, but...'

She bent and stirred again with her finger. Steam swivelled off the top of the water.

'What about now?'

She just used magic to warm up my water. I know that in light of all that had happened it should not have surprised me, but it was not like making elephants disappear or flying over the Grand Canyon. It was useful magic. Domestic magic. And it had been unexpected.

I hesitantly tested the temperature of the water. 'It's perfect.'

She stood up straight and looked at me.

'Thanks,' I added. I hoped it hadn't come too late. I felt vulnerable standing there in nothing but boxers and so close to her in that little space.

She continued staring. There was no emotion on her face, unless extreme lack of interest counts. Apathy. It certainly wasn't the emotion I wished to evoke. I was conscious of her missing soul.

I didn't want her to hear me bring up the matter of her missing soul. I had to block my mind to her, but I didn't know how. Could she read my mind? Was she reading my mind and listening to me thinking that I had to stop her from reading my mind? How had I managed to block out Brother Moses? Why had he been trying to read my mind in the first place?

A terrible thought occurred to me. What if I hadn't managed to block out Brother Moses? What if he only said I did so I wouldn't know he was reading my mind? Something from the night before had disturbed me about him. What was it? I remembered. How did he know about the coin? His explanation wasn't really an explanation. But no. That wasn't it. That wasn't the only thing. There was something else nagging, tugging, calling my attention to what I was missing.

My shoes.

That was it. The missing shoes. How did he know about Titus Titus making people take off their shoes before they got onto his spaceship?

A cold shiver spread goosebumps over my body. In my flat, both Brother Moses and Adesua had taken their shoes off and placed them on the stool.

Adesua continued staring at me.

Chapter 28

Omo Pidan Pidan

The sight of captives being led to execution has always baffled me.

Why do the condemned go willingly to their death? What is going on in their minds? Why don't they fight? Why don't they struggle? Why don't they plead? Why don't they try to escape? Getting dressed up as Mr Magic evoked those images and made me wonder what I would do if it was I being led to the slaughter.

I did not trust the people I was with. I did not know what their true intentions were. One thing alone was certain, there was fatal danger ahead, but all I could do was play along and play my part until the end they had planned for me. There was no escaping them. There was no beating them. I was being led to the slaughter, so I, like all those fated people being escorted to the noose that would soon be around their necks, followed the directions of my executioners with obedient subservience and I understood why the others don't run.

Back at the glasshouse, Brother Moses had tried to explain how everything was a dimension. He said that every human concept, notion, feeling, was a dimension all of its own. What we named, he said, was the murmur of

191

the dimension hidden to us. As such, weight was an entire dimension. Love was also a dimension too, and even joy was its own dimension. He told me of a dimension in which the inhabitants experienced gravity as déjà vu. In another, he said, time was sensed, just as we smell wet soil before the rain reaches us.

He assured me I would discover my own dimension, the first of many that only I would be able to access and the discovery of which would make me a most grand magician, like my father.

Getting ready to go on stage to perform magic tricks for a crowd of village kids, I felt I had discovered my first dimension.

I felt a bond with every man, woman, and child before me who had faced the countdown of a firing squad, approached a hangman's noose, been led to an altar dripping with blood, or faced a cross on which they were to be strung. The hopelessness that paralysed their will stretched across continents and through millenia, connecting each and every one of them. Every one of us. I knew I had discovered something so powerful, so profound, yet so hopeless, for what magic tricks could be learnt from hopelessness?

Brother Moses was done with the fireworks and he was entertaining the kids with oversized playing cards that vanished in one palm and appeared in the other. Adesua was in the truck looking at me, her hands on the steering wheel. Next to her, sitting very close, Rachel also watched me through the dusty windshield, and with a steeliness reminiscent of the brutal vagueness which I'd come to expect from Adesua. Oddly, it reminded me of my mother.

'Are you ready?' Brother Moses said. His cards vanished from his clasped palms. The children applauded.

I nodded. He waved at Adesua. The engine of the big car roared to life.

'Follow me,' he said.

I followed. The children followed. Adesua drove slowly behind me, my manager, and my new fans. Under the morning sun we marched, to the cheer of the children and chants of 'omo pidan pidan'.

'What does pidan pidan mean?' I asked. I knew enough Yoruba to know what omo meant. Child.

'Magician,' he said.

I looked at the kids. They were clapping and skipping, holding hands and repeating the chorus, 'omo pidan pidan'.

'They're calling me a magician's child?'

'Yes.'

'How do they know that?'

'They can read.'

Once more he had managed to give me an answer that was less than an answer. I searched around us for what he meant and found it behind, slowly keeping up with us. I moved out of the lorry's way and let it gain on me. On the side of the lorry was a painting of a magician dressed in a black suit and a black tie, holding a black hat from which red block letters grew out accompanied by orange sparks: Mr MAGIC! Beneath the painting of the magician was the proclamation: SON OF THE MOST AMAZING GRAND MAGICIAN IN THE UNIVERSE!

I let the lorry move further past me. I caught Adesua's face looking at me in the wing mirror. On the back of the lorry the magician's gloved hands were spread above the body of his levitating assistant, floating perfectly straight at waist height, her arms crossed over her belly, her eyes shut. Under this image was written: AMAZING MAGICAL DISPLAYS. Whatever that meant.

I moved to the other side of the lorry. This painting was of the magician, his female assistant, and a man dressed in purple. The faces didn't look like us, but there was no doubt who they were meant to be. In front of the magician was written in two lines, OMO PIDAN PIDAN ATI AWAN OSERE RE. The letters were accented but the marks meant nothing to me so I did not dwell on them. I recognised the word, ati, so the sentence up to that was, 'The magician's child and'. I guessed the remainder to be 'his assistants'.

I looked into the cabin through Rachel's side but I couldn't see her as she was sitting so close to Adesua. I continued round the lorry, going full circle until I had rejoined Brother Moses in the middle of our escort party. Perhaps they thought he was the magician and I was the helper.

'What exactly do you expect me to do?' I said. 'You know I don't know any magic, right?'

'Don't speak so loud, Master Osaretin,' he said. He looked at the children. 'You know magic. You just don't know that you know.'

'You think I will get in front of them and suddenly know how to do magic?'

'Yes. Something like that. Don't worry about it. You'll be fine. And your assistant will be there.'

'What did she tell Rachel?'

'Everything.'

'What do you mean, everything?'

'Everything. She has to come with us so she can be safe. She would soon learn who we really are. Better to tell her now.'

'She told her about the magic?'

'Everything. Magic, your father, who you are, why there are people looking for you. Everything. She has to know everything so we can protect her.'

'Are you protecting her or are you just interested in finding out what happened to us on that man's space-craft?'

'We are protecting her from him.'

We walked a few more paces without talking. I was sure he wasn't reading my mind or he would have seen the next question coming.

'What has this got to do with my mother?'

As I expected, it caught him off guard. He looked at me

without his smile and walked into a little village boy skipping along in front of him, almost knocking the child over.

Chapter 29

What Itohan Knows

'Why do you ask about her?' a startled Brother Moses said.

He was shocked. He was surprised. For once I could see past his effervescent smile into a person who was unprepared and uneasy and perplexed all at once.

'Did you know her?' I asked.

It had all suddenly come together in my head in an instant, and in that same instant I had realised what a weapon it was if I played it right. The pieces had been there all along: the behaviour of my mother following my father's death, her failure to mourn, how detached she was from me, the unapologetic curiosity with which she studied me when I caught her watching, the fact that Brother Moses was friends with my father yet never mentioned my mother.

'I know Itohan,' Brother Moses said, 'but this has nothing to do with her.'

'You said Titus Titus will use the people I care about against me.'

'Your mother can take care of herself.'

'Why? Is she one of us?'

'No.'

'What is she? A witch? A mermaid? An alien?'

'She is something different.'

'Different? How?'

'Just different. Master Osaretin, there are things we do not know that we are better off not knowing. Leave Itohan out of this.'

'She's my mother.'

'Yes, yes. But this is not her problem. She has done her part.'

'Her part? You mean she knows about all this?'

He looked away. He began to talk to a kid who had been trying to catch hold of his hand. I stopped walking and pulled his shoulder so that he was facing me.

'What do you mean she has done her part?' I asked again.

Adesua honked. We looked at each other through the dirty windscreen where the wipers had thinned out the dust. This time it was I who looked away as if she were nothing.

'Tell me what you mean,' I said.

'She gave birth to you.'

'Yeah. So?'

'So her part is done.'

'I don't understand.'

'And I don't expect you to. Once your training is complete you will understand everything. No one will have to tell you anything. You will know things even I do not know. That is why we are here. Remember what I told you about the dimension in which all things are possible?

The one that can only be accessed through the imaginations of others? It is there that you will begin to discover everything, including yourself. You want answers? Well then, focus on what we are here to do. Focus on your training. Mesmerise these children, and if you succeed you will see their minds opening up to you and expanding your own.'

I knew he was trying to distract me from the question. I knew there was more to my mother than he was prepared to tell me. I also knew that there was no way I was going to get the truth from him by simply asking. I had to think of another way.

Adesua pressed the loud horn again and gestured to me.

'Does my mother have a soul?' I said.

'What?'

I had startled Brother Moses again.

'You said my father once entered the dimension of death.'

'Yes.'

'What was he doing there? Did he go to get her soul back?'

'I already told you, Master Osaretin, nobody knows why he went there.'

'Nobody?'

'Well, maybe one person.'

'Who?'

'Itohan.'

'My mother.'

'Yes. Your mother. His wife and assistant.'

'She was a magician too. I knew it.'

'She was more than that.'

'What else was she?'

'I think you have to ask her that yourself. Can we continue walking now? We are keeping everyone waiting.'

Adesua was about to press the horn again, so I looked at her. Her hand hovered over the steering wheel as we eyed each other. I had known what she was about to do before she did it. Her surprised look confirmed that it wasn't just coincidence. Just like I could predict the coins and hide my thoughts, I was also able to see into the future. Or had I merely read her mind?

Chapter 30

The Village Doctor

It turned out that where we had spent the night was some sort of outpost. Half a mile down a road that cut through the forest, we arrived at the actual town of Faka fiki, and it was a real town.

The forest had been cleared, and streets and houses had been built where wild animals once roamed. The houses were not glorified huts like the bungalow we slept in, they were two and three storey buildings painted in the brightest colours – sky blue, yellow, bright green, pink – and they had elegant gardens that stretched out to wide sidewalks. Each garden was unique with its own variety of flowers and ornamental trees.

There were trees with all yellow leaves and others with all purple leaves. And the grass was the greenest I had ever seen. On the driveways of some of the beautiful houses, SUVs, sport cars, and other luxury vehicles were parked. There was a blood red Maserati; a silver Mercedes coupe; a white Lamborghini. What was this place? Who owned the cars? In one driveway there was a black Harley Davidson leaning on its stand. My brain refused to see Odedina or any of the men from the night before owning any of the luxury cars or the big houses.

The kids ran ahead of us on the cobblestone road lined with streetlights, chanting, 'Magic, magic.'

'What is this place?' I said. 'How come they are so rich?'

'They are hunters and farmers, but that is not where their wealth comes from. A long time ago the women who first settled here discovered something that made them very rich. So rich that the money is still bearing interest to this day, enough for every child of Faka fiki not to ever have to work.'

'What did they discover?'

'Only the women know. They pass the secret knowledge from mother to daughter.'

'What could it be?'

'Ask Itohan. She might tell you, since she didn't have a daughter.'

'Wait. What? My mother? But she's Edo.'

'Yes. But her mother was from here and she herself lived here when she was a child. That is why you are safe here.'

'She never told me that.'

'Did she tell you she was Efosa's assistant?'

My mother could not be from this town. No disrespect to the inhabitants of Faka fiki, but she was five foot eight.

'Look, they have come to meet us,' Brother Moses said.

We had come to a roundabout at the end of the road.

A concrete dolphin balanced on its belly with its tail up in the air was pouring water out of its mouth into the palms of a mermaid sitting next to it with its tail curled upwards. Even in Lagos I had never seen a fountain so beautiful. Behind it was open land. Behind that the forest spread out. A group walked up from the road to the left of the fountain. In front were the short men, in jeans, shirts, and baseball caps. Behind them were women as tall as my mum. At the centre of the women was one with a white wrapper round her chest, coral beads round her neck, and a crown on her head. The crown was blue and appeared to be made of stiff cloth. It fitted tightly around her hairline, fanning out like a flat-topped cone. It had two lines of white cowry shells around it. Set into the shells were large gems of various colours.

How was it that the women were tall and the men short? The children all looked the right size for their age. Was it something to do with the secret the women had discovered? Were the male children playing around me destined to stop growing at some point while their female playmates continued to grow past them to become such tall women?

The adults lined up in front of us. The children mingled among them. Odedina was in the front row in a pair of brown linen trousers and a white short sleeved linen shirt. He smiled at Adesua in the lorry.

The queen wasn't that old. She was about Brother Moses' age. I wondered if there was a king. She looked at

Brother Moses and I could see the recognition blossoming on her face.

'Moses, is that you?'

Brother Moses stepped forward with his arms spread out. They embraced and rocked each other back and forth as the rest of us watched. They separated but still held each other's hands. She looked into his eyes with the fondness with which special friends look at each other after they've been apart for a very long time. He smiled a smile that I'd not seen before.

'Moses, Moses. Why did you sneak in like a thief? Why didn't you send word that you were coming?'

'It has been a long time. I didn't think you would remember me.'

'How could I forget you? You were the first magician I ever knew.'

'You are queen now.'

'Yes, I am queen now. And you are still performing. I'm glad you changed your mind.'

She held his hand up to her people.

'This man is our friend. He came here with his magic show when I was a young lady. They were here when we had problems with the banks. One of his young magicians was an accountant; he looked into the accounts for us. Another one was a lawyer; she represented us in the court case. They all helped us. They did it free of charge. And this one here, he had just got his scholarship to go and study in England, but he stayed with us for a whole year and helped us until we won the case. They are our magician friends that the old people talk about. Without them, the banks and the government would have taken all the money from our accounts that they froze during the civil war.'

She turned to Brother Moses.

'Why didn't you say who you were? You could have been turned back last night. We have been having problems with foreigners lately.'

'Is that why you have the warnings outside?'

'You saw them? Youth coppers keep trying to get our girls pregnant and pastors keep trying to collect money for their church projects. We are having a tough time keeping the city people away. There are too many bad people around these days.'

'They showed us a hole in the roof.'

'Oh, that.' She laughed. 'When the government posts male coppers here, that is the place we give them to stay. We show them the hole so they will be afraid to touch our girls.'

'So, spirits didn't snatch up any youth coppers through the hole?'

He was looking at me when he said it.

'You of all people know that is not possible. You told me that there is no real magic. Oops. I shouldn't say that out loud.'

They both smiled. There was definitely something in the way they looked at each other.

Adesua had climbed out of the lorry. She stood beside Brother Moses. Odedina walked up to her and did his handshake that was dripping with swag. I looked about for Rachel. I found her behind us. She was standing close to the lorry, her shoulders hunched and arms folded across her body, and she was staring at me with a forlorn look on her face. As I was about to go to her when Brother Moses started introducing me to the queen.

'This is my new apprentice, the amazing Mr Magic. He will be performing today. And this is his assistant, the amazing Adesua.'

We shook hands with the lady.

'And who is that one?' the queen asked, looking at Rachel.

'That is his girlfriend,' Brother Moses said. 'She travels with us when we are on the road.'

My eyes darted to Adesua as he said it. She also looked at me. I wasn't sure if it was in reaction to me looking at her.

Brother Moses waited for Rachel to walk over and take his waiting hand then he presented her to the queen.

'Rachel, meet Her Royal Highness, the Queen of Faka fiki. Queen Modupe Adeola.'

'Is anything the matter?' the queen asked Rachel. 'You don't look too well.'

We all held our breath waiting for her answer.

After an uncomfortable few seconds of silence, Rachel said, 'It's nothing. I mean, I think I'm coming down with something.'

'In that case I will ask our new doctor to see you. He arrived this morning. Just like you people he was sent by the government. They sent us a white doctor. Can you believe that? His first name and his surname are the same. Dr Titus Titus.'

Chapter 31

The White Death

Rachel gasped. Her knees gave as she fainted. The queen, Brother Moses, Adesua, and I all reached out to catch her. It was a tussle between Adesua and me after the others had left Rachel in our arms, but Adesua eventually also let go and I alone bore the weight of Rachel's unconscious body.

'Oh dear, oh dear,' the queen said, 'we really must take her to the doctor now.'

Adesua and I looked at Brother Moses. He spoke for us.

'No, no. That won't be necessary. She just needs some water. She's very tired, that's all.'

'Let me be the judge of that,' a male voice spoke from behind us. I recognised the voice and went weak with fear as I turned to look. My arms lost their strength and Rachel began to slip from me. Adesua caught her just in time and helped me secure my hold on the limp body in my arms.

Titus Titus walked up to us, his hands folded behind his back. A man and a woman followed him closely behind. They were dressed in the white tops, white trousers, and white shoes of nurses' uniforms. The man was tanned and looked well built under his clothes. His blonde hair was in locks that scattered over his shoulders and he had light stubble across his chin. The woman was Asian. Her silky black hair was pulled tightly from her face, with just a few loose strands drifting over her forehead. She looked like a no-nonsense kind of person, the way she looked straight ahead without blinking or moving a single muscle on her face. They all had their hands behind their backs.

Titus Titus stopped in front of me. He looked at Rachel.

'Looks to me like we need to take her back with us to the clinic,' he said. His companions unclasped their hands and moved out from behind him. He stepped back, so that they stepped in front of him, ready to take Rachel from me. There was no way I was letting them take her. The woman reached for Rachel. I swung away from her. Like a cat, she hissed at me. I looked at her. Her eyes were un-blinking. She hissed again, but her lips didn't move. It was in my head. She was hissing at me in my head. I growled back at her. Her eyebrows raised. I saw the surprise in her eyes. I had broken the stillness of her face. I was in her head too. She hissed again, and I, like a lion with its head raised to the sky over its territory, roared. A single sound had not departed from my still face but the force of my roar lifted the strands from her forehead and blew them back over her head. She stepped back and looked at Titus Titus. The man stepped back as well. Titus Titus came forward to try to take Rachel from me. He brought his tattooed fingers close to her body. I showed him the lion

I had become. He snatched his hands away and locked them behind his body.

Looking up, he said, 'I better not touch her. Nobody should touch her. She might have the same illness that took out your former doctor and his staff. These two must be quarantined now.'

The townspeople stepped back.

'What happened to your former doctor?' Brother Moses asked the queen.

'They all fell ill last night. We found them all unconscious in their clinic. We had to break down the door. We took them to the magnetic garden but it didn't help. Luckily this morning the new doctors arrived. That is why the men were dressed like that last night.'

'Yes. The magnetic garden is not as strong as it was when I was a child. Then, it could rip your earrings from your ears and bury them so deep in the soil you wouldn't be able to dig them up. My mother talked about a time when it would draw the iron from a man's blood through his skin. Long before then, it swallowed men whole. But is has been getting weaker as the years have gone by. It still heals, but it has become so weak it couldn't heal the doctor and his nurses.'

'Where are they now?'

'We left them there, under the shade of an Agogo tree, so that the flowers would sing to them. We are hoping the garden can still heal them.'

'What time did you find them at the clinic?'

'About nine o'clock.'

'Do they normally work that late? No.'

'Isn't it strange that the doctor and the nurses fell ill last night and this morning new ones arrived?'

Titus Titus answered. 'Like I told the queen, before the doctor passed out he managed to contact the Global Centre for Disease Control and Prevention. One of his nurses had visited a neighbouring town. While there he treated a sick infant. He must have picked up the disease and brought it back here with him. The doctor knew that he had become infected along with the rest of his staff. They all gathered in the clinic and locked themselves in there so they wouldn't infect anyone else. They are heroes.'

The queen continued. 'Dr Titus Titus and his staff are experts on infectious diseases in sub-Saharan Africa. He thinks he's seen this before. He said it's called The White Death.'

'White Death?' Brother Moses said.

'Yes,' Titus Titus said. 'The white death. I don't name these things, I just treat them.'

'And how is this White Death contracted?'

'Who knows? It's a new one. We are still doing studies.'

'Shouldn't you be in the town where the sick child lives?'

'Another team is already there.'

'Yes? Ok. How can our friend be sick with your disease?'

'My disease? My disease?'

Titus Titus held his hands out and swivelled round to his companions. With over-enthusiastic incredulity on his face he spoke to the queen: 'Your Majesty, who are these clowns? If they don't co-operate with us, I'm afraid they're going to spread this virulent disease all through your kingdom. A public gathering with lots of people is exactly what we don't want right now. You cannot let them do their magic show till we know they're not sick. The little children, the aged, and the infirm will be first. Soon it'll take hold and there will be no home left untouched. We have to quarantine these people, at least until we know what's wrong with the girl. There is no cure for The White Death. I don't want to die. Do you? Do you want your subjects to die? They must not do the show or else people will die.'

The queen might not have heard it but Brother Moses, Adesua, and I got the message. The people of Faka fiki had become hostages, but they didn't know it. Titus Titus believed I was Mr Magic. He believed I would discover it when I performed for the children. He would sooner kill the townspeople than allow me to become more powerful than him. He was afraid of me.

'I will go with him,' I said.

Chapter 32

Through Innocent Eyes

Brother Moses placed a hand on my shoulder and shook his head.

He said, 'You are not ready.'

I had never felt more ready in my life. I did not know exactly what I was going to do, but I knew what had to be done. I had to protect everyone, including Rachel, and the only way to do so was by going with Titus Titus and his accomplices. It was me they wanted. But when Brother Moses looked at me with an expression that was a mixture of pride at my bravery and pity that I did not know to be rightfully afraid, I considered my lack of a plan and felt really, really stupid that I had offered to sacrifice myself. Let's face it. I might have roared like a lion, but these people knew real magic. They lived on the moon, for crying out loud.

Rachel moaned. I renewed my hold on her. It was the first sign of life from her, apart from the steady breathing I'd established when I placed my finger under her nose. She began to stir. The last thing I wanted was for Titus Titus to be the first person she saw when she woke up. I swung around with her body in my arms and it was as if Adesua had read my mind. She took Rachel from me even as her feet and hands began to search for the ground and for a point of reference.

Titus Titus and Adesua exchanged snarls that no one could have missed, then he looked at me and said, 'Well then, let's go.'

The queen stepped forward. 'The girl is ok. It can't be The White Death. You said the victims never recover.'

'Maybe it's not, but we still have to be cautious, you understand?'

'We will take her to the magnetic garden, just in case.'

'Do what you like, but he still has to come with me.'

'Why?'

'Because no one here is safe if he doesn't come with me.'

'And why is that?'

The men slowly panned out and surrounded Titus Titus, his sidekicks, and me. The queen had clocked that there was something amiss and so had her subjects. Odedina in particular had been paying close attention. He stood closest to the queen. His fingers were formed into fists.

I felt Brother Moses looking at me. He nodded, even though I didn't know what he meant by it. He moved away from the townspeople and joined us in the circle the men had formed.

'And now, the Amazing Mr Magic will perform his first magical spectacle for us,' Brother Moses declared. He spoke as if the circle was a stage. He held his hand out to me as if I should know what to do. I didn't.

Titus Titus threw his hands up. 'Your Majesty? Really?'

The queen was as surprised as he was. As I was, for that matter.

She looked at Brother Moses for an explanation.

'He must not do any magic here,' Titus Titus said through gritted teeth.

Brother Moses addressed the crowd. 'You have all come out to see a magic show today, haven't you?'

The children in the crowd cheered.

'Well then, a magical extravaganza you shall see.'

He thrust his hands in the direction of the lorry. A puff of blue smoke shot out of his sleeves, rose and expanded in the air, obscuring the vehicle and drawing gasps from the audience. As the smoke thinned, the back carriage of the lorry unfolded and retracted under the vehicle, revealing a small red and gold structure on the back of the lorry. It was a little shed with a single door and no windows. The walls were red and the door and the domed roof were gold. Golden stars of various sizes swirled around the bottom half of the structure.

Brother Moses clapped at the audience and they clapped too.

'Mr Magic,' he said. 'Mr Magic,' and it became a chant that the children picked up and clapped to with vigour and with excitement.

Brother Moses nodded at me and swept his hand towards the stage.

I looked at Titus Titus. His snarling face dared me to go up. I looked around.

The children clapped and chanted, 'Mr Magic, Mr Magic.'

It all became clear to me. I had to become Mr Magic if we were to defeat Titus Titus. The only way to become Mr Magic was to perform on stage and we were running out of time. I walked to the lorry. The crowd followed behind. I began to climb onto the back. I looked up and Adesua was already there waiting for me. She reached down and pulled me up.

'Where is Rachel?' I said.

'They've taken her to the magnetic garden.'

'Why?'

'The garden heals. Come with me.' There was urgency in her voice. She took my hand and led me into the red hut.

It was dark inside. All around the walls there were narrow tables covered in red cloth that also covered various objects on the tables. I couldn't make out from their shapes what they were. I thought the inside was bigger than the outside.

'Take off your clothes,' Adesua said. She took off her hat, pulled her scarf away, wiggled out of her coat and started unbuttoning her shirt.

'Hurry. Take off your clothes now.'

'Why?'

'Just trust me.'

She threw her boots aside and pulled her tights down. She looked up at me still fully dressed and she looked pissed.

'Now,' she said.

I began taking my clothes off. She waited for me to finish. I dropped my shirt on top of the rest of my clothes and stood in front of her in my boxers. I saw that she had taken off her pants and bra.

'Everything,' she said. 'We have to be quick.'

I hesitated. 'Now,' she said. 'Why?'

'Now.'

I bent down, pulled my boxers down and stepped out of them. I threw them onto the rest of my clothes, put my hands over my groin, and looked to the side so as not to look at her. .

'Don't panic,' she said. 'Look at me.'

I looked into her eyes. I tried to decode the new look on her face. There was something soft, or kind, or gentle in her eyes. She was almost apologetic. With our eyes still locked, she took one big step forward so quickly that she would have made both of us fall over backwards as I didn't have enough time to ready myself for her weight. I froze in place as my brain tried to decide whether to brace for the fall or make a late attempt to catch her in my arms. But she didn't crash into me. Air was sucked out of my lungs as she stepped right through me. I did not feel a thing, except a temporary sensation of being off-balance, which was probably due to the reflex reaction to get out of her way.

I heard her feet on the ground behind me. 'Don't panic' wasn't enough warning for walking through a person.

I turned round and looked for the edges of the mirror that was not there, for I was looking at my naked self looking back at me with a straight face. I was standing in front of myself! I was looking at myself and it was not like looking into a mirror. This was a real flesh and blood, breathing, seeing, hearing, feeling person, with my face and my body, standing in front of me. Another me before me. 'Don't panic' was definitely way, way, way too insufficient to prepare me for this.

Then I thought, 'If she is me, who am I?'

I held up the backs of my hands before my eyes and they were hers. I looked down at myself and saw breasts from an angle I had never seen them before. I brought my hands, her hands, to my breasts, her breasts.

'Don't you dare,' she said with my voice.

My hands froze.

'Get dressed. We have to be quick. They're waiting.'

Indeed the children were chanting and clapping for Mr Magic, but unbeknownst to them they had been cheated out of the most fantastic magical feat they could have witnessed.

I looked around.

'Are you searching for a mirror?' she said. It was disconcerting to hear myself talking to me.

'Yes.'

I sounded like her.

'Don't. Mirrors are not your friend. I will perform in your place this time. No one else but you and I will know it. All you have to do is smile and do whatever I ask you to do on stage. Do you remember why we are doing this?'

'To learn magic.'

'To use their imagination to see beyond. When their minds open. What should I do?'

'Just watch. When you see it, you will know. We are running out of time.'

Chapter 33

One False Start

In my body and dressed as me, Adesua walked out onto the stage.

The children's excitement exploded and they screamed in one roaring, joyful voice, 'Magic!'

They were eager to see me perform. They would see Adesua perform.

Brother Moses was on the stage. I looked at him expecting him to look at me but he nodded at Adesua instead before he turned to the audience.

'Queen, ladies, gentlemen, children, I present to you, the amazing, the fantastic, the exciting, the marvellous, the dazzling, the one, the only, Mr Magic!'

Brother Moses raised his hands. Orange sparks flew from his sleeves. The audience clapped and the children screamed as if he was a rock star. Then, fireworks still pouring out of his sleeves, he turned his back to the crowd and stood on the edge of the little stage. He winked at Adesua, and without warning he crouched, swung his hands backwards over his head and he leapt into the air, did a double backflip, and landed on the ground in front of the queen. The children loved it and they clapped even louder and screamed. The adults were also impressed and they too clapped. I wasn't sure if he had managed the feat by magic or by athleticism.

Titus Titus was in front glowering at Adesua, his accomplices by his side. He really didn't know she was me and I was her.

Adesua, or rather, 'Mr Magic', pulled the tip of a black cloth from inside his jacket and the cloth kept coming out and coming out until it was the size of a large blanket.

Mr Magic spread the blanket out in front of him, raised it up to his neck, smiled at the audience, then raised it further so it covered his entire body. I was watching from behind. Mr Magic stepped back and dropped the cloth and the shape of a box formed under the material as it settled down. Wasting no time, Mr Magic snatched the cloth away to reveal a big black box that had not been there before.

The children cheered.

Mr Magic held the cloth to me. I rushed to take it and then I remembered to smile. Holding the black material, I wondered what to do with it. I folded it neatly while still smiling at the audience who, thankfully, were concentrating on Mr Magic.

I found myself looking for Rachel in the crowd, even though Adesua had told me she'd been taken to the magnetic garden. As Mr Magic performed his tricks, I imagined what the magnetic garden was. What made it magnetic, how come it could heal, and why was it losing its power?

White doves flew away from Mr Magic's hands. I remembered that I should be watching the people for when their imagination opened up some sort of channel for me. This was the whole point of being in Faka fiki.

A drop of water fell upon my forehead. I looked up and blinked as another drop fell onto my eyelid. It was the wrong season for rain. I looked at Brother Moses. He was beaming at Adesua. I looked at Titus Titus. He was staring at me. I got the feeling he had been looking at me for some time. A satisfied smirk was on his face. A drop of rain fell before my eyes and splashed at my feet. I looked at the sky again. The clouds were in motion, swiftly gathering over us and blocking out the brilliance of the morning sky. I looked at Titus Titus. His smirk became a grin. He too looked at the sky and held out his palm. I saw the single raindrop hit his hand. He grinned widely as he looked at me and he nodded and kept nodding. He wanted me to know it was his doing. He knew that Adesua was me and that I was her.

The sky darkened even more and the clouds let fall their rain. The townspeople covered their heads with their hands and ran in different directions, each to their homes. The show was over and I had learnt nothing. I was no more of a magician than when we started. Adesua's soul depended on me learning magic. Rachel's safety depended on me learning magic. The lives of all the townspeople depended on me learning magic.

Chapter 34

Like Father Like Son

'What was that?' Brother Moses asked again, but Adesua and I knew not to answer. He turned away from us and continued to march back and forth in his wet purple clothes in the living room of the queen's guest house which was to be our new home. Adesua and I stood side by side as ourselves and in our dry normal clothes as he grew angrier with each step he took.

'What were you thinking?' he said. 'What made you do it? This was his one chance and you blew it. You just don't want to believe in him, do you? You refuse to believe. Now see what you've done. Titus Titus knows everything. He knows he's not ready.'

'I thought it would work,' Adesua said.

'You thought? You thought? No. You did not think. It was his show. His show. If you had been thinking you would have remembered that. How is he going to learn anything if you keep doing everything for him? How?'

He was being hard on her. Her only thought had been for me. She had lost her soul protecting me; it was my turn to protect her.

'She was only trying to help me,' I said. 'I wouldn't have been able to do anything up there on my own.'

'I'm coming to you. You, this is the last time you pull a stunt like this. Got that? You have almost cost us everything. Everything. And you, when are you going to start believing in yourself? Who told you that you wouldn't have been able to perform without her help? Did she tell you that? Do you think I would have allowed you to go up on that stage if I didn't know you could do it? Why do you think Titus Titus is here? To watch a charlatan? To capture a pretender? He is here because of you. You. He has come to get you, and the only way I can protect you is for you to protect yourself. You have to become who you are.'

'Why doesn't he just take me?'

'Precisely. Why. I'll tell you why. Because he is afraid of you. What if you try to capture a sleeping lion and it wakes up? He knows who you are. He believes in you even though you don't believe in yourself. He wants your powers for himself. He wants you on their side and to accomplish this he must corrupt your mind. He wants to turn you. It is safer and a million, million times more rewarding for him than the risk of trying to kill you. Do you get it? Don't just nod at me if you don't. Do you get it or don't you?'

'I don't.'

'Adesua, you try.'

Brother Moses walked away, throwing his hands about over his head. He sat down heavily on a sofa and let out a long gasp. His body collapsed as his spirit deflated

228

and the anger on his face gave way to sullenness.

Adesua spoke gently, cautiously. She was afraid of him, or she was still beating herself up for making the mistake of performing in my place. I still didn't see how that mattered.

'We haven't told you everything,' she said. 'It is not just your father who predicted you. Every other grand magician who has reached the same level he reached has had the same vision of Mr Magic but only your father recognised his face, because it was the face of his son.

'All the other grand magicians on our side also believe you are the one, but no one knows what it means. We are not sure if you are one of us or one of them. If you join them, they will have the advantage of your power and the Great Schism will be over. They will have won.

'They will reveal themselves to the world. They will use their powers openly. They will become gods walking the Earth.' Brother Moses spoke with a sunken voice. 'Slaves and masters. Everyone you know, your friends, your cousins, your colleagues at work, your friends from kindergarten, your teachers, your neighbours, they will all become slaves. It has happened before, when the great pyramid was built. A handful of men and women turned the entire population of the world into slaves and made them build the pyramids. They want to do it again. They just need a magician like you on their side.'

Adesua's demeanour and voice remained subdued. She touched my arm.

'It is important that you learn how to protect yourself,' she said. 'I'm sorry I did what I did today. I wouldn't have done it if I knew it wouldn't help you. I made a foolish mistake.'

'It's not your fault,' I said to her. 'It is not her fault. Have you guys even considered that maybe I am not Mr Magic?'

Brother Moses looked at me. 'You learnt to stop your mind being read and no one taught you how to do it,' he said. He stood up. 'You roared like a lion and those minions backed down.' He began walking towards me. 'You looked a powerful magician in the eyes and you said you would follow him.' He stood close to me. 'Do you know why I didn't tell you how to use the time machine?' I stared blankly back at him. 'Because I don't know how. Your father gave me that ball. He showed me how to start it, but he didn't show me how to use it to travel back. I asked and he said, 'When the time comes, you will know what to do.' I thought it was a gift from him to me, but no, I was wrong. It wasn't for me. That is why he didn't tell me how to use it. It was meant for you all along. And when the time came, I knew that you would know what to do.

'Only one magician had ever travelled back in time. That magician was your father. Now there are two.'

Chapter 35

God's Eye View

'If you don't know it by now, I'll tell you. There is no such thing as magic. Not in the way people imagine it to be.'

Brother Moses walked to the window. He lifted the curtain and looked up at the sky. It was still dark outside and the unseasonal rain hadn't stopped.

'This rain, it's only magic until you know how he did it. When you learn the secret of how it's done and you can do it too, it's no longer magic. My tricks, the cards in my sleeves, the things I keep in my hair, you can do all of those things. You just have to know how I do it. Did you know that there is no space too small to hold an entire universe? You can keep an entire galaxy in the fold of your palm. Think about that.

'But the vanity. Oh, the vanity. We look down on the plants. We don't say sorry when we step on the grass. We fish the oceans. They're not sentient, we tell ourselves. They don't feel. They don't think. They are not like us. We are intelligent and they are not. We are great and they are small.

Yet we are all stardust. The same matter in me is in the fish and in the grass. Atoms. And in an atom there could be a whole new world.

Civilisations could exist in the tiniest bits of us. Entire worlds could be clinging to a single blade of grass. We mow the lawn and end a million worlds and we don't even know it. We don't think anything of it.

'Yet we are atoms too. We also live in a world so small it fits on the tip of a needle of another world. All of us. Our entire planet. Our entire solar system, on the tip of someone's needle. Think of it.

'We are nothing. Our minds tell us otherwise, but our minds are foolish. We are nothing. Knowledge is such a burden.'

He had been speaking facing the window. He shook his head and when he turned, he had luminescent tears running down each cheek, like galaxies escaping from his eyes.

He was crying stars and telling me magic was not real. My eyes were fixed on his glistening tears. He walked up to me until he was really close. His brow was furrowed as if he'd seen something on my face that shouldn't be there. He looked into each of my eyes in turn, over and over again, as if he was searching for something. All the time his face was squished with puzzlement, almost as if he was confused, or surprised.

'Maybe I was wrong,' he finally said. 'Maybe we've all been wrong. It has happened before that we've all been wrong. But I was sure this time. I was so, so sure. Maybe Efosa misled me. Maybe Efosa was misled himself.'

'What do you mean you've been wrong before? Was

there another Mr Magic?'

'We thought it was your father.'

'My father? Why?'

'He was the greatest, grandest, magician ever. We thought he had the God's eye view.'

'God's eye view?'

'Yes. He could see everything from all dimensions. He could see the beginning and the end of all things. The God's eye view.'

'How do you know he wasn't the one?'

'Because he saw you before you were born and he was afraid of you. But maybe he was wrong. Maybe he made a mistake.'

He shook his head and turned away. Adesua watched him. From the look on her face I guessed she was filled with empathy for him. She looked to me and it felt as if her eyes were begging me to do something. I had nothing.

'Brother Moses,' she said, 'you can sneak away with him now. If anyone comes, they'll find all three of us. You can train him at Snake Island. Or somewhere far away. He hasn't had a chance. Just give him a chance. Let him try.'

Brother Moses shook his head. 'It's no use,' he said. 'I chose this place because if something were to happen to him here, the magnetic garden could heal him. Even I had my doubts, you see. Now I know it. Mr Magic would have been able to heal himself.

'I'm afraid we are left with just one option. We have to let Titus Titus know that he is not the one. Maybe then he'll let him be, and the girl too. I must return to the glass-house at once and tell the rest that I've been wrong.'

'What happens then?' I asked.

'You don't have to worry about that. You won't remember any of this, I'll take care of that. I promise. You'll return to your life as it was before we interrupted you.'

'And what will happen to Adesua's soul?'

'Her soul? I'm afraid that is lost forever. But that won't be your concern. You won't remember any of this. It'll be like none of it ever happened. Your conscience won't bother you. Spaceships won't take you up. Bad magicians won't come looking for you.'

'A minute ago you were so sure I was the one, now you're telling me to just forget everything? What made you change your mind?'

'It's your eyes.'

'My eyes?'

'Yes. They are just like his.'

'Who?'

'Efosa. Your father. You have the same eyes. You have his eyes. His exact eyes. The very same eyes he had.'

'What does that mean?'

He walked up to me and looked into my eyes. 'Efosa, are you in there? You found a way to come back, didn't you?'

'What are you talking about?'

'You have latent knowledge. You can do things you shouldn't be able to do. Did they tell you the circumstanc-

234

es of your birth?'

'What circumstances?'

'It doesn't matter now.'

'You can't just say stuff like that then tell me it doesn't matter. And what makes you think I want to forget everything? I want to help. If I have my father's powers, then I can help.'

'But you are not Mr Magic. You are Efosa. He saw Mr Magic and he was afraid of him.'

'He saw me. I am Mr Magic.'

'You don't understand. Efosa saw him, but Mr Magic made him think it was his son he saw. Mr Magic tricked him. The real Mr Magic is out there and we are wasting time here. That is what he wanted. Don't you see? He sent us on this wild goose chase so we wouldn't know to search for him. Your father was powerful, and Mr Magic, coming across him, would have known this. For all we know, he is watching us right now.'

'The real Mr Magic?'

'Yes. Keeping us in sight. Keeping an eye on the only magician that can challenge him.'

'Me? Keeping an eye on me? No. On Efosa.'

'If I am not Mr Magic, then who could it be? I don't know.'

I didn't know what to think. I stared at him and he stared back and Adesua stood silently and watched the two of us. She never believed I was Mr Magic; now more than ever I wanted her to. I suddenly thought of Rachel.

That was someone else whose safety depended on me being Mr Magic.

'Where is Rachel?' I said.

Chapter 36

The Real Mr Magic

I had seen flying magicians, a woman standing before me in my own body, an umbrella that deflected bullets, even a UFO, but I did not know what to expect of the magnetic garden, and I wanted to know its secrets.

Brother Moses went to the queen to seek her permission to enter the garden to see our friend, Rachel. Only the people of Faka fiki knew the way there, and only their men were allowed to go into it. That was why the men were short while the women were not. The strength of the garden had stunted the men's growth.

The queen would do anything for Brother Moses; he needed only to ask her. I already knew there had been something between them many years ago, even if that something was never explored or spoken about or allowed to blossom when it first had the chance. But the something lingered and could still be sensed, even if only in the spontaneous smiles and restrained looks of two people who were unable, unwilling or not bold enough to be who they were meant to be together. She gave her blessing to our intrusion into their secret garden.

We had to take off all our clothes and wrap white cloths of linen around our bodies.

Three men from the village would lead us there. Odedina, being one of our guides, repeatedly asked Adesua to check for rings, even after she had shown her fingers and pulled her earlobes for all to see. He kept asking anyway, every few steps, as if he were reading from an instruction manual that told him to repeat the question several times.

'I do not have any metals on me,' Adesua eventually said with finality and a dab of anger. It was then that Odedina explained the danger of leaving a metallic object on the body. He said, 'The magnetic garden will tear earrings from your ears, and any other rings from any other places.'

Adesua responded with a simple, 'Oh.' She assured him that she didn't have any piercings. None whatsoever.

Odedina smiled and nodded. I wanted to tell him that I knew she didn't have any piercings.

The men led and we followed, all of us in white, all of us naked under the linen, all of us getting drenched in the rain Titus Titus had conjured.

From the time I'd voiced the thought, an urgency had gripped us all and set us in motion, so that we hadn't had time to discuss and debate the merits and otherwise of my proposal. And so we walked in silence through the rain, each one of us, magicians and magician in training, weighing the implication of the serendipitous inkling I'd had, namely that Mr Magic was Rachel.

But had we talked about it, I would have counted on

their magical senses to understand a secondary inference I'd since happened upon. The only way Rachel could be Mr Magic was if I wasn't Mr Magic.

There was more than one reason that thought of her had risen to the top of my consciousness when Brother Moses suggested that the real Mr Magic would do good to be shadowing me, and my father in me. Rachel was in danger.

Titus Titus wanted her, not my father. He could not afford an unpredictable fight with me, but he could handicap me before the battle began, by securing a keepsake that I would fight a million battles or lay down all my weapons for. Titus Titus was Mr Magic all along. I dared not tell the rest, in case they abandoned the quest to rescue Rachel.

Chapter 37

A Walk In the Rain

'Isn't that your friend with the doctor?' Odedina said and pointed.

At the end of the road, a hundred metres away, Titus Titus was walking away from us and he was holding Rachel by her arm. Like us, they didn't have umbrellas, but unlike us, they were not shielding their faces or hunching their backs to the rain. They turned by a yellow house with red roof tiles and they walked out of view.

'Rachel,', I shouted.

Neither of them looked back.

I was about to run after them but Brother Moses held my hand and said, 'No.'

'Why?' I asked.

'It is not good to run in the rain,' he said, looking into my eyes with a straight face. I understood that he meant something other than what he'd said and he expected me to understand it or at least accept his instruction to me not to run after the magician who had Rachel.

We walked on but with quicker steps. We rounded the corner and saw Titus Titus and Rachel ahead. Adesua held my hand so we both dropped back behind the rest.

Speaking quietly she said, 'You must be careful. People

must not know who we are.'

It took a second for me to realise she was explaining what Brother Moses meant when he said no and he held me back. What did he think I would do? Fly?

'We can only do magic on stage or else they will call us witches,' she said. 'They will hunt us and they will kill us. They outnumber us. It has happened before.'

Titus Titus turned by another house. A bright green one this time, with blue roof tiles and a purple door. We got to the house not long after them. Behind the house was a long garden backing onto the forest. The houses had no fences, so each garden led to the neighbour's. Titus Titus and Rachel were at the end of the row of gardens that made the block. It was impossible for them to have walked that far, unless they were running, and it was as if he had waited for us to catch up so we'd see where he turned next. With Rachel firmly in his grip, he walked out of the garden to the side of the house, and once again they were out of sight.

'They are going in circles,' Brother Moses said.

The village men began to sprint after them. I jogged past them.

When I came to where we'd last seen them, they had walked halfway up the road where we'd first spotted them and he was about to turn left this time, just after a row of five houses that backed onto the forest.

I shouted her name, 'Rachel.'

Still, they didn't look back. I waited for Brother Moses,

Adesua and the men to catch up with me.

'Where are they going?' I asked Odedina.

He looked at me but he did not answer. His face was creased with worry.

'Is that the way to the magnetic garden?' I asked.

He looked up at me again. I knew the answer.

'That's not them,' I said.

Brother Moses and Adesua looked at me.

'It's not Titus Titus. And it is not Rachel. He did what you did. That is the Asian girl and the white Rasta guy.'

I saw on Brother Moses' face the instant he also figured out what I already realised. Adesua was as unreadable as usual.

I turned to Odedina. 'Where is the hospital?' Titus Titus already had Rachael. His assistants were only keeping us busy while he got away.

Odedina was torn between keeping his eyes on the two figures walking further away and giving me instructions.

Adesua took charge. 'Odedina, you have to take us to the hospital, now. The girl's life is in danger.'

Odedina looked ahead to where the two had disappeared. His confusion was understandable.

Adesua bent down to him and placed her hands on his shoulders.

'Listen to me,' she said. 'That man is not a doctor. He is something else. He is evil. Those two are his assistants. They are also dangerous. If we don't get to the girl now he will do something terrible to her.'

She only managed to confuse him more.

'Just trust me and take us to the hospital, please.'

Odedina looked at the empty road. When he looked back at Adesua he jumped and screamed and his mates had to catch him from running away. Whatever scared him, only he saw. She leaned to him again and placed a hand on his shoulder.

'You see now? That is how they did it. Now, take us to the hospital before it's too late.'

Chapter 38

Dragon's Breath

The town of Faka fiki turned out to be really quite big. We passed several brightly coloured houses, a church, a mosque, a school with a large football field by its side, and even a building that looked like an office block. The further away from the centre we got, the fewer the houses became, and the taller the trees that surrounded them.

The men led us to one such isolated house in the middle of a clearing in the forest. Several metres away from the building, the townsmen stopped on the narrow road leading to it. Amazingly, it was not raining on that particular stretch of road, or the clearing it led to.

Odedina pointed. 'There,' he said.

'You'd better go now,' Adesua said to our escorts and then she stepped out in front of the rest of us and focused on the house ahead.

The men turned back and ran. We walked on to the edge of the large clearing. The building was about twenty metres away.

'Can you see them?' Adesua said, looking at the house.

Brother Moses took out his phone from his afro and held it to the house as if to take a picture. I looked at the screen and saw an x-ray of the house. I also saw move-

245

ment on the black and white image. I leaned in closer. I was looking into the building. A figure was climbing up the staircase. In his arms he carried a limp body. It was Rachel. It had to be.

Titus Titus suddenly stopped on the stairs and paused. He placed Rachel down and began to descend.

'He knows we're here,' Brother Moses said, 'and he's got her.'

'What's he doing?'

'He's coming out.'

'Where's his ship?'

Brother Moses moved his phone to scan above the building. He moved the phone higher and we saw it. Up above the house, just above the height of the trees, a massive, bright white disc spun slowly and silently, emitting a mist that clung to its body and swirled with it as it turned. It was so bright that it was uncomfortable to look at it too long on the screen of the phone. I had to look away. I looked above the house.

There was nothing there. I looked at the screen and there it was again, spinning slowly, its brilliance something like looking at the sun.

The front door of the house opened but there was no one there.

Brother Moses put his phone back into his hair. Both he and Adesua stepped forward. He held his hand out to stop me following suit.

Titus Titus walked through the open doorway and out

246

of the house. He stopped after just a couple of steps. The smirk on his face made him look like evil personified. He seemed pleased with himself.

'Up to your old tricks, Moses?' he said. 'Spying on a fellow magician? Isn't that against your magician's code of conduct? Isn't that forbidden, brother?'

'We have come for the girl,' Brother Moses said.

'So you have. Let's see, one, two, three of you. And there's just one of me. Hardly a fair contest, wouldn't you say?'

With the fingers of his right hand, he flicked the back of his left hand. The bees tattooed onto his hand slipped off like black paper cut outs, then turned into real bees. He dropped his hand to his side and shook it. Bees poured out of his sleeve and circled his feet in a dense mass that kept growing. He raised his hands and thrust them at us. The bees flew towards us, buzzing.

With both hands, Brother Moses parted his afro in the middle and turned the crown of his head to the approaching bees, holding both halves tightly apart. White smoke poured out of the gap in his hair. The smoke moved like a living thing. It spread out to block the path of the approaching bees and curled inwards to envelope them. Any bee that tried to escape was caught by a tongue of smoke that flicked out like a hungry lizard. When all the bees had been captured, the smoke rose like a cloud, shifting and swirling as its prisoners tried to escape. It rose and rose, up and up, past the trees and into the sky above, and kept ascending into the heavens.

'Impressive,' Titus Titus said. 'Now, just how much can you fit into that hair of yours? I bet they didn't let you empty your pockets into that ridiculous toga. Let's see what you can do with these.'

Titus Titus pulled his right sleeve up, exposing a forearm covered in black tattoos. With his left hand he scraped at the tattoos from the elbow down. Scorpions peeled off his arm. Thousands of them scattered onto the ground and started scampering towards us, their venom-laden tails hanging over their backs.

Brother Moses dug his fingers into his afro and searched. The scorpions kept coming. I was stepping backwards and so was Adesua. As if he was sitting on a stool, Brother Moses raised each leg off the ground, hunched forward, tucked his head into his knees, and wrapped his hands around his folded legs in mid-air, and just continued folding into himself until he folded away from sight. Without any noise or fuss, he just vanished. A moment later, out of thin air, he unfolded behind Titus Titus, silently stretching out his limbs until he was standing behind the evil magician. He began to pull out a long glistening sword from his hair.

Grinning devilishly, his eyes on me, oblivious to Brother Moses folding out behind him, Titus Titus ripped his shirt apart. He had a huge, coiled dragon on his chest. The beast began to uncurl itself. It lifted away from his skin and took on a glimmering red colour. It flared its red nostrils and blinked its scaly eyelids over its green and black reptile eyes. Its wings unfolded as it grew in size to several metres wide. With one flap that swept the scorpions off the ground, it climbed above its master's head. The beast turned in the air. It dipped its head to Brother Moses and bellowed out a jet of fire so intense I felt the heat on my face from where I stood.

Brother Moses had begun to fold away before the flame reached him but Titus Titus swung round and caught one of his ankles, holding him in the dragon's fire.

Adesua ran at Titus Titus and did a sliding tackle through the scorpions. Without fuss, Titus Titus lifted the leg she aimed for and she slid under his foot. He casually stepped on her belly, pinning her down with his foot. She kicked and grabbed at his leg but she couldn't move him an inch. With fervour, the scorpions began swarming her.

The dragon hovered above, tree branches blowing as it flapped its massive wing and belched out fire onto Brother Moses' leg that Titus Titus had seized. Adesua was beneath Titus Titus' foot, brushing off scorpions that had completely covered her body and struggling to breathe under the pressure of the magician's foot. I stood, feeling the heat of the dragon's breath on my skin, and the anguish of my friends in my heart.

There was nothing I could do to save them.

A Sister Woma...

Chapter 39

A Super Woman

The red dragon continued to hover above Titus Titus, flapping its wings and breathing down fire onto Brother Moses' leg. The scorpions climbed over each other on top of Adesua's motionless body under Titus Titus' foot, and Titus Titus looked at me, grinning mockingly as he killed my friends.

I could have run. He would have sent one of the pestilences tattooed onto his skin after me, but at least I would have died running rather than standing there watching my friends die and not being able do anything. But I stayed and I waited, not knowing what for.

I looked up at something in the sky that had caught my eye. Or did I know to expect it? In the distance, tearing a fiery path through the clouds, a tiny shooting star was rushing down from the heavens.

It was coming in fast. It got bigger quickly. It was a person flying in.

They were coming in too fast. They flew in over the red dragon's wings and landed somewhere between me and Titus Titus, the velocity of their approach carrying them onwards along the ground, tearing a path into the soil as they slid to a stop, inches from my feet.

I recognised the combed back, shoulder length black hair, the ankara blouse and the long wrap. But it couldn't be. Still crouching, she looked up at me. Her eyes were as impassioned and unreadable as they had always been. Without a word or any kind of acknowledgement, or even hint of the slightest awareness of how she had just freaked me out, she stood up and turned to face the carnage.

The dragon filled its lungs. She held her hand up at it and the beast coughed black smoke.

'Itohan,' Titus Titus said. He looked surprised.

He let go of Brother Moses. The charred smouldering limb vanished and a puff of smoke marked where it had disappeared. He threw off his ripped shirt. Tattoos slid round from his back onto his chest, peeled off his body and charged at my mother. An army of warriors with bodies covered in scaly, reddish exoskeletons, and armed with axes and clubs and daggers.

My mother held out her arms by her sides. Long shimmering swords grew out from both hands. The charging army slowed down and formed into two straight lines. On each side of her, the warriors took turns walking though the blades, slicing themselves in two at the waist as they did so.

Titus Titus stepped off Adesua. The scorpions climbed over each other to reach his hand. They rushed onto his arm and settled down onto his skin as tiny black tattoos. The dragon shrank and snapped onto his chest and coiled back into place.

The swords retracted and my mother's hands formed into fists.

Hunched forward she marched towards Titus Titus. At first he held up his hand as if to stop her, then he took one step back, turned around and ran into the house.

My mother ran after him and I ran to Adesua.

'Mum, wait,' I shouted as she was about to enter the building.

I was on my knees by Adesua. Her skin was covered in reddish bruises where she'd been stung. She was motionless but breathing with difficulty, making a rasping sound that was painful to listen to. But she was breathing.

'We have to help her,' I said.

With her hands on the doorframe, my mother looked at Adesua for a second then she turned back to look into the house, up the staircase where Titus Titus had escaped. Rachel was still in there, but Adesua was dying. I couldn't let her die again, and especially without her soul.

'Mum, please.'

From about the height of my head where I knelt, and about a foot or two away, out of nothing a hand stretched out, followed by another. Then Brother Moses' head emerged, and his torso, and one leg, and finally the burnt leg. He groaned when his injured limb touched the ground.

'Itohan,' he said.

My mum looked at him.

He limped and groaned as he knelt by my side next

to Adesua.

My mum let go of the doorframe and walked to us. As I watched her, and as my eyes pleaded for her to help Adesua in whatever way she could, her hair stretched up, straight away from her head. So did Bother Moses' afro. From where she lay on the ground, Adesua's hair curved around the sides of her face and rose straight up towards the sky. I felt a tingling on my own scalp.

I looked up. Above the house the ship had become visible. It was metallic grey and it rotated slowly. Evenly spaced white lights lined its rim. Rows of light stretched from the edge to a large circle of bright white light in the middle.

As we watched, light poured out from the belly of the ship and fell onto the top of the building. The light was like a liquid current that flowed downwards on its outer surface and upwards in its core. Titus Titus rose through the light, Rachel's lifeless body in his arms. They went through the white hole into the ship, then the current of light fell away, collapsing into the building as the ship rose slowly away. It came to a silent halt for a brief moment, then it suddenly shot straight up into the sky and vanished from sight.

My mother's hair fell back into its normal sweptback style. She watched the ship go, then she turned her attention to us, first inspecting Brother Moses's leg then slowly sweeping her eyes over Adesua's body.

She bent down and picked Adesua up as if she weighed

nothing, and held her to her body with one hand. Next she offered her other hand to Brother Moses. He limped over, grimacing, and put his hand on her shoulder. She held him tightly to her body.

'Do you know the way to the magnetic garden?' she asked me.

'No.'

'Can you fly?'

'No.'

'Did anyone see you do magic?'

'No. Only on stage.'

'Go back to town and tell them to take you to the garden. We will be under the Agogo tree.'

She turned her face to the open sky above the clearing and lifted off the ground, Adesua and Brother Moses in her arms.

Chapter 40

Stabbed in the Front

I ran into Titus' assistats on the road back to town. We all stopped when we saw each other. They were still pretending to be Titus Titus and Rachel, but I knew that they knew that I knew. The one that was the magician turned back into the woman and the one that was Rachel became the dreadlocked man. They slowly began to back away. They were afraid of me.

'He left you behind,' I said. They stopped their retreat. 'And he took my friend.'

The man spoke. 'We didn't know what he was up to, man. We were only doing what he told us to do. You've got to believe me, man.'

'What are you going to do with us?' the woman said. 'What is your name?' I asked.

'Yun.'

'And you?'

'Simon.'

'Are you gonna let us go?' the woman said, 'or are you gonna kill us?'

'Mr Magic is no killer,' Simon said. 'Right, bro? I mean, you're like all good 'n' all, right? This whole thing, it's just a mistake, you know. We thought we were coming to meet you. To learn stuff from you. When we got to this place, that's when he told us what he really wanted to do. We had no choice. He was gonna kill us.'

I relaxed as Simon talked. Yun saw the change in my demeanour and hissed, showing her clenched teeth. She ran at me, leapt, and in the air she morphed into black puma. I stepped aside and her claws missed my neck. She landed and tumbled behind me. She scampered onto her paws and hissed at me. I thought out loud, 'I have no time for this.'

'Get lost,' I said.

I swept my hand at her as if to shoo her off. A gust of wind blew from my gesture, lifted her off the ground and threw her several metres through the air and against the trunk of a tree. She fell to the ground and got onto her paws. She looked at me, turned, and bounded away into the forest.

I turned back to find Simon was right in front of me, with a dagger clasped in his hand. He jabbed at my chest, driving the dagger into my heart. I looked down. Blood flowed down my chest to the white linen round my waist.

'Sorry, bro,' he said, 'but I can't leave you alive or you'll find us and kill us. I don't wanna die, bro. It ain't personal, just common sense.'

Chapter 41

For Fear of Men

The puma scrambled to its feet and disappeared into the vegetation. A branch sprang back into place.

'I was going to let you go,' I said.

I turned and caught Simon's hand, still clasped around the handle of the dagger. The tip of the weapon bent a strand of hair on my chest. The look of surprise on his face turned to panic. He couldn't drive the blade forward into my flesh and he couldn't pull his hand away. I watched the effect of pain on his face. First, tiny vessels in his hands began to burst, then his bones cracked and continued to fracture. The pain travelled from his hand to his wrist, up his forearm to his shoulder, and then into his heart. He fell to his knees, his hand still in mine, being steadily crushed, his other hand futilely trying to pry my fingers apart. His mouth remained open in a mute scream. I had no pity for him. I had seen what he meant to do. I had felt his blade cut through the soft tissue of my heart. I had seen him do to me what I was about to do to him.

The soles of my feet tingled. I could hear ants moving in their anthills, birds picking at their nests, snakes gliding over the dead leaves of the forest around us. I could hear a caterpillar munching on the edge of a leaf on the other side of the forest, and a snail crawling on its belly onto the road, beyond the signs warning people to stay away from Faka fiki.

From the vibrations my feet detected, I could tell how far away the people of the town were. They were coming for us. They had clubs and stones, and in their hearts they carried murderous intentions which quickened their stride.

I understood Adesua's warning concerning people. I understood why my mother asked me if anyone had seen me do magic. The people of Faka fiki had learnt our secret and become afraid of us. To them we were wizards and witches able to harm them with our magic, and there was only one way they knew to deal with such beings. It also became clear what Adesua meant when she said they outnumbered us. It wasn't the sheer combined physical force of an army; no army, however large, could be big enough to defeat the ingenuity of one able to call forth fire breathing dragons. It was the collective force of their will. Together, united in fear and purpose, they had become more than just the sum of the parts, and the resultant excess was a formidable opponent in the face of any force known to man.

Simon's hand was seconds from turning to pulp in my grip. I pushed down on him, forcing him into the ground until he was buried up to his waist and unable to escape. I wiped my bloody hand clean on his locks and I took to the sky.

Chapter 42

Into The Magnetic Garden

How can I describe flying? It feels normal. Why can't you fly? You need only do it. Don't try; just fly. It is natural, but our brain in its default mode just doesn't know it.

I flew in whatever direction I wanted to go. If I wanted to go faster, I did. If I wanted to slow down, I did. I didn't need to think of it, or concentrate on turning right or turning left, like you don't need to think of placing one leg in front of the other when you walk, you just walk. I neither felt weightless nor propelled by an invisible force. I wasn't carried by unseen hands or buoyed by a special current. I just flew because people can fly. They just don't know it.

From the sky the world looked different. I wasn't as high up as a plane and I wasn't going as fast either, so I could notice things. I saw the faces of the people who looked up and pointed at me. I saw the disbelief in their eyes. I saw the chained dog that winked at me and went back to sleep. I saw the deflated, sun-faded balls on the roofs. And when I flew higher, I saw the place I was searching for. A circle of colours in the middle of a green forest.

I landed behind a wall of ancient Iroko trees. They

were close together so that their trunks had fused and their branches mingled high above, forming a seemingly impenetrable circle several kilometres wide, with no obvious passage through into the enclosed garden. With the great wall of trees behind me, I took in the strange garden. The soil was black and it sparkled in the sunlight, as if it had a million tiny diamonds in it.

The trees were much shorter than the surrounding forest and no two of them were alike. Their trunks were slim or thick, smooth or rough, grooved or thorny, a single colour or an entire rainbow. The leaves were every shape and colour you could imagine. Some were triangles, some were perfect circles. Others were like two leaves fused together down the stem. Between the trees, otherworldly plants grew with strange flowers, each petal a different colour. Patches of tall grass grew in clusters as if they had been planted specifically where they were. The blades of grass grew in every colour: green, black, yellow, blue, purple, and some were transparent.

There were no dead leaves on the ground. I couldn't hear a bird singing or an insect crawling. I walked into the garden. I passed between a white tree with yellow leaves on my left, with purple buds shaped like prisms, and on my right a tree with a grey trunk, translucent leaves and shimmering black flowers. On its trunk I found the insects I had not heard.

White soldier ants the size of bees, marching up and down with glasslike bites of leaves in their beaks.

I came to a lake I had seen from a distance. I had to get close to believe what I had seen from afar. The water was as clear as water in a cup. At the bottom of the lake pebbles of different colours lay close together, and above the water, twelve inches from the surface, fishes of different sizes, colours, and shapes swam and interacted in the open air as if they were in the water. There were small fishes the size of a finger, larger ones as big as my forearm, and some as large as a dog, all swimming using their fins and their bodies to paddle and turn as if they were in water. But they were above the lake.

'Osaretin,' my mother called.

I turned to her.

'I saw you coming,' she said. 'Follow me.'

She was not surprised that I had managed to fly. The expression on her face was the same detached one I had learnt to accept as just the way she was. I had just watched her chase dragons away and make a strong magician flee, but judging by her face and her voice, and her coolness that was as unnerving as always, none of it meant more to her than anything else that could be in her mind at any time. I followed her in silence through the fantastic plants of the garden and towards the soft sound of a hundred bells.

The Agogo tree had a smooth, shiny, black trunk about six feet wide. It looked like polished marble. It reflected our images as we approached. The fat trunk was also quite short, and at first I thought I would have to bend to avoid its jet black leaves shaped like tongues made of marble. Its branches spread wide, covering a large area of ground beneath it. The sound was coming from its round black fruits that hung in clusters like grapes. I thought the sound was made when they clinked against each other but I could detect no motion, yet they rang softly like bells of various tones, and they made an ever-changing melody.

Beneath the tree, on the soft black soil, Brother Moses, Adesua and four other people I did not know lay in foetal positions.

The bruises had vanished from Adesua's body. Brother Moses' leg was no longer burnt. I could see no injuries on the bodies of the other people. But it was Adesua I was most concerned about.

'Will she be ok?' I asked.

'Yes,' my mother said. 'And Moses. But it's too late for the others.'

'Can she hear us?'

'No. They are asleep. They need to rest for the garden to repair them.'

I watched Adesua's face. I tried to detect her breathing. Her palms were together under her head as a pillow.

'You really like her,' my mother said.

I nodded.

'What happened to her soul?'

'You can tell?'

'Anyone can tell.'

'It was my fault.'

'I see. And you want to get it back for her?'

'Yes. If I can learn how to.'

'If she allows you to. What about the other girl? You want to save her?'

'Yes.'

'She's not like us, you know that?'

'Yes. I know. We work together. It's my fault she got mixed up in all this.'

'I see. Do you know where he has taken her?'

'To the moon?'

'If you go there, you might not return, and if you try to get this one's soul back, you could die.'

'Are you asking me to choose who to save?'

'Which one are you ready to die for?'

'Why can't I save both of them?'

'Why can't you? There is no reason at all.'

Chapter 43

Taken In The Night

My mother sat on the ground and rested her back on the smooth trunk of the Agogo tree.

I sat beside her, and slowly rested my bare back upon the trunk, expecting it to be cold like the marble it resembled, but it wasn't. It was neither warm nor cold, perfectly matching the temperature of my own body.

I had so many questions for my mother, but I knew I had to ask the right ones. She had a habit of getting bored with me. Since I was a child she would only indulge my inquisitive nature for so long. A point was always reached, and the length of getting to that point varied, when she would suddenly be done and either stop answering or outright tell me to go and read my books. It got worse after my father died. Then, she hardly had time for me even though it looked like she had given up everything for me. She would not let me ask any questions, stopping me before I finished speaking. And even when she had questions for me, she would answer them for me. Are you hungry? Yes. You shouldn't be. You've had too much to eat today.

'What happened when I was born?' I said.

'I went into labour, I pushed you out, they cut the umbilical cord.'

'Brother Moses asked if I know about the circumstances of my birth.'

'Well then he should have told you.'

'Mother.'

'Ok. It is not about your birth. Your birth was ordinary. I was in labour for fourteen hours. I was glad to get you out of my body. Nothing special. He was talking about something else your father told him.'

'What is it?'

'When I was a little girl in this town, I used to be taken onto a ship like the one you saw. It always happened at night and always when I was alone in my bed. The light used to come through the wall. A man would come and take me up into his ship. No one believed me so I stopped telling them.

'The man taught me everything. From a young age I could do some amazing things.

'I was five when he started taking me onto the ship. It didn't stop until I was twenty-one. Just before I met your father. I was three months pregnant with you when I met your father. Your father's people knew. That's why they've never accepted you.'

'Who was my father?'

'Don't be silly. You know who your father is.'

'But you said you were pregnant before you met him.'

'Your father did not recognise me when we met, but I knew who he was. He was the man on the ship. The man I was with, three months before I met him.'

'I'm confused.'

'So was he. Your father is the only man I've ever been with. There is only one of him. He is your father. You don't need to understand. You just need to know.'

'Did he know I was his son?'

'You look like him, don't you?'

'Did you tell him?'

'I didn't have to. Something happened to him after we married that made him know all he had to know.'

'What happened to him?'

'I don't know. Ask him when you see him.'

'But, he's dead. He is dead, isn't he?'

'If you can exist in any dimension, will you stay here?'

'Where is he?'

'Everywhere. When you find him he will answer the rest of your questions.'

'Mother?'

'Yes?'

'Who am I?'

'You are my son.'

'People say I am Mr Magic.'

'Then that is what they say. Have you decided?'

'Decided what?'

'Who you are going to save.'

'I can save both of them.'

'Do you know how to get her soul back?'

'No. Not yet. Do you?'

'No. It is not for me to do. I can take you to the moon.'

'I can fly.'

'Not to the moon. Don't be silly.'

'How would we get there?'

'He left his ship. When I was little, he taught me how to fly it. He said he would leave it for me in case I needed to use it one day.'

'Where is it?'

'It's been here hundreds of years. It's what makes this garden magnetic.'

'It's here?'

'Yes. It's in the lake. We should go now, if you really want to get her back.'

'What about them?' I looked at Brother Moses and Adesua sleeping silently. The villagers had seen me fly into the magnetic garden. They were on their way to lynch the witches and wizards.

'They will be fine.'

Chapter 44

Afternoon Trip To The Moon

My mother stood up and began to walk out of the shade of the agogo tree. She stopped and turned to look at me. I recognised the look on her face from my childhood, when she would stare at me blankly and soon after be satisfied with whatever action I took to appease her in interpretation of her look.

I got up and she continued walking. I could hear the villagers; they had just arrived outside the wall of Iroko trees. I followed my mother to the clear lake whose fish swam over the surface of its water. She knelt by the edge of the lake and placed her hand into the water. The fish swam away from her in a frenzy. She watched the water but nothing happened. A minute passed and she kept her eyes on the water, and still, nothing happened. One at a time, the armed villagers were passing through a thicket at the bottom of the wall where a narrow passage though the great trees was hidden from view.

My mother continued staring at the water but nothing happened. The men were gathering at the mouth of the passage inside the garden, waiting till they were all through then they would come for us. I remembered the queen saying that the garden had gotten weak. My mother said it was the spacecraft that made the garden magnetic. Perhaps its battery had drained out. The men were matching into the garden now.

'Mum,' I said, but she kept staring at the water, then the fish became excited. They swam in an agitated fashion, turning and turning again, and they began to leap several feet into the air, landing again where they swam above the water. The surface of the lake rippled in concentric circles that spread out from the middle. The fish gathered at the edge of the water. The ripples intensified in frequency. The entire surface of the water began to vibrate so fast that drops started to dart up. The pebbles at the bottom moved as if they were being pushed apart. They gathered at the edges of the lake. A metallic ship rose from the exposed sandy bottom and broke the surface, water washing off its smooth body. It kept rising and spinning slowly, the lights on its underside glowing white. When it was about twenty feet above the water it stopped and hovered in place. I heard the footsteps of the men as they ran though the magnetic garden with their cudgels and their deadly fear of what they thought we were. They had seen the spacecraft. They knew we were at the lake.

From a circle in the centre of the ship, light shot out at an angle and fell at our feet on the bank. It was the same strange, alive-like light I had seen Titus Titus and Rachel rise up through. My mother took my hand and stepped into the beam just as the first of the men began to arrive at the lake. I held my breath and also stepped in to the light. In my belly I felt I was falling, but in reality we were rising weightlessly up through the light. I couldn't hear anything but it was not silent, rather it was as if the sound waves hitting my ears were so strong they blocked out everything including themselves. After a few moments I felt solid ground beneath my feet and I swayed as gravity reaffirmed its force on me and the light dissolved away around us.

We had been taken into the spaceship. Everything inside was a colour I can only describe as silver. It was not silver, but a new and different colour I had never seen before and that I do not have a name for; but from the way it was reflective and neutral and unlike any other colour, I can only describe it as silver.

You could see through the entire top half of the ship, but it was not like looking out through a window. You could tell that you were looking through the solid metallic material of the ship. It gave the world outside a sort of greyish metallic hue. Looking closely you could see where the panels of the dome met and even the circuitry and the technology inside. The lower half of the ship was opaque. We were standing in the middle of the floor, but there was no evidence of the opening through which we had been transported by the 'organic' light, and the inside of the ship was not spinning. Four smooth 'silver' chairs that were more like curved chaises longues were arranged in a circle facing inwards towards each other.

They were perfectly still but they had no connection

to the ground or the walls. They just floated in fixed positions in space. They were shaped to fit the outline of a person lying down. There was a ridge to separate the legs. The armrests were cut into the surface, and led to indentations for the palms and fingers. All the chairs were the same size. They were built for people much bigger than us.

My mother climbed into one of them. As she rested her palms in place, the metal began to move and close in on her, forming a perfect fit for her body.

'Get in,' she said.

I began to climb into the next chair. It was solid and cool. I adjusted my body in the oversized space and laid my palms into the indentations.

The chair moved against my body. It gently moulded around me till I was snugly secured in its grip, lying down facing the sky, my heart beating with excitement and fear.

'Remember to breathe,' my mother said.

I did not feel the ship moving, but the clouds in the sky above steadily got more and more sparse; then there were no clouds, only blue sky. Then there was no blue sky but a blackness that spread and filled the dome of the ship.

'Look,' my mother said.

The ship tilted and light appeared at the edge of the darkness. It was the Earth, scrolling up before my eyes, a radiant blue body with a thin white hue clinging to its curvature. I had seen pictures of the Earth from space, but a picture could never capture the awesomeness of its beautiful sharp glow in the vastness of black space speckled with more stars that I had ever seen. From that distance, Mother Earth dominated the universe. She truly looked like the centre of everything. As we sailed further away, the blue and brown of the oceans and the continents beneath white swirls of clouds became less distinct until the Earth hung like a marble ball in the blackness of space.

Our world slid away from my view. The stars above me grew dim, until they became lost in the darkness.

My mother sat up in her chair. She got to her feet and stood watching me.

'Are we there yet?' I said.

She nodded.

I did not know how to get out of the chair. I began to lift myself and the metal relinquished its snug hold on me.

My mother walked to the wall behind her chair. She stretched her hand to the metallic body of the craft and it opened like the shutter of a camera. She reached in and pulled out a grey, rubbery looking suit. It had legs and arms that ended in feet and gloves. The suit had a hood made of the same material, and the hood had a face with two large, golden oval eyes which reflected everything. There were no other features on the suit, no pockets, no belts, no zippers, nothing. I did not know how it could be worn.

My mother removed her wrapper and her blouse and dropped them onto the floor of the spaceship. She held the suit by the shoulders and it opened up along the back. She stepped in and it shrank around her body, clinging to her like it was her skin.

She faced me. She looked like the grey aliens in UFO movies. I could see the ridge of her nose and the outline of her ears but there were no holes in the suit. She turned her palm to me and I imagined her blank look under the suit, expecting me to understand what she had refused to adequately communicate.

I got my own suit out from behind my chair and put it on the way I had seen her do, feeling the material wrap itself against me.

'This will protect your from the moon's radiation for up to forty days,' my mother said.

It sounded as if she was in my suit with me.

'I can breathe,' I said.

I had been anxious over how breathing would be possible in the suit.

'Yes,' my mother said. 'The suit will give you up to forty days of oxygen.'

I held my hands before me and looked at them through the golden lens. They appeared white. I looked up at the dome. Above me was only darkness. I did not understand why the moon was so dark.

'Are you ready?' my mother asked.

'Yes,' I replied. '

She took my hand.

Chapter 45

Red Eye Speaks

My mother and I stood side by side in the centre of the ship. I held my breath as I waited for something to happen, watching the silvery floor beneath our feet with suspicion. The muscles of my legs tensed as I anticipated a hole materialising beneath us and I tried to resist the urge to jump away. Nothing happened, and we continued to stand in silence. I looked at my mother. She still hadn't let go of my hand but even with her spacesuit on, I could tell that she wasn't looking at me at me. She stared blankly ahead, her thoughts as unreadable as they had always been.

As I studied her profile, my eyes were drawn to tiny sparks of white light bursting out of nothing around us. The silent sparks multiplied and swirled. In a few seconds we were enveloped in a column of light and I could not see beyond the whiteness that surrounded us. I looked down and there was no ground beneath my feet, just brilliant white. I held my mother's hand tighter, but we were not falling. We were suspended in place in the light, and it was the light that moved, not us. It swirled round and round in an upward pattern. I looked up to where the current of light was leading, and felt the firmness of the ground beneath my feet.

My mother let go of me. I looked down as the light broke away into sparks that gradually died out. The ground was grey. I raised my leg and my body swayed gently to one side. I grabbed my mother's hand again. I steadied myself and watched dust rise from where I'd placed my foot back down. I looked around. We were in a crater the size of a football field. About forty feet deep, and with a slope that looked impossible to climb. Beyond the crater was darkness. I looked up. Our ship was silently spinning above our heads.

'There are two things you have to know,' my mother said. 'He knows who you are, and he knew you would come.'

'Who else is here?' I asked.

'On the beautiful side of the moon, a colony of magicians like him. There used to be just three, but now there are more. No one knows how many. And they want you to join them.'

'Why are they on the moon?'

'You've learnt of the Great Schism. Before that there was the Great War. They lost and they were banished from the Earth so they came here. They want to return. If they succeed, they will make slaves of all humans. Come.'

She took my hand and stepped forward, pulling me with her. Our feet left the ground and we were afloat for a second. I felt I had to keep going or I would tip over. We took bouncing strides until we were facing the grey, dusty slope of the crater. It was as if the entire surface of the moon was covered in sand and rocks.

'One more thing,' my mother said. 'You cannot believe anything he tells you, no matter what he says.'

She let go of my hand and watched me. The alien eyes of her spacesuit transmitted the familiar intensity of her stare. I looked up at the wall of rock. It was impossible to climb or bounce out of the crater, and somehow I knew that I could not fly on the moon like I could on Earth. A three-foot wide square of rock lifted off the face of the wall before us. It moved outwards then pivoted up, revealing a dark hole beneath it. A reflective black sphere the size of a football floated out of the hole. I saw myself, my mother, our ship, and the crater, all curved around the glass – like surface of the ball.

A thin blue line formed across the front of the sphere and separated like eyelids. Beneath the eyelid was silver and it had a large red 'iris' in the middle. The red expanded and contracted as if focusing on us. The sphere turned to me. I felt the eye looking at me. It turned to my mother. The voice of Titus Titus spoke from it.

'Itohan. What a surprise. Twice in one day. We really should stop meeting like this. And I see you've brought the tenderfoot with you. Itohan, Itohan, you of all people know the rules. You cannot be here.'

'This is as far as I go. I want the girl.'

'And why would I give her to you?'

'Take my son. He is the one you want.'

Chapter 46

Lost in A Crater

I looked at my mother. She did not turn to look at me.

'Mother,' I said, but she did not answer.

I could not believe she had offered me in return for Rachel. When she said she could take me to the moon, I had thought it was just to get Rachel back. Trading my life for hers had not been on the table. Maybe that was what she meant when she said I might not come back if I went to the moon. She knew she would have sacrifice me to get Rachel back.

'Mother,' I said again. She was looking straight into the red eye. Her alien-like appearance in the space suit suddenly made it feel like she was truly another being; one with no care or concern for my safety. But beneath the grey suit was my mother, and she wouldn't leave me to die alone on the moon. She must have a plan, and one that didn't involve my death. She was playing a trick on Titus Titus. He would release Rachel to her and we would all escape on my mother's ship.

'Your son for an ordinary girl?' Titus Titus said through the eye. 'Yes.'

'You know the rules, Itohan. You cannot break them.'

'I know.'

'If you do, the truce is broken and your dear humans will pay.'

'I know.'

'I give you the girl and you give me your son?'

'Yes.'

'No tomfoolery now. You take the girl and leave, and I keep him. Right?'

'Right.'

'Why then, we have deal. You can have the girl.'

'She must not be hurt in anyway.'

'Ah ha! Now I understand. The girl is fine. You lose.'

The eyelid closed over the red eye and the black sphere floated back into the hole in the wall of the crater. The lid closed over the hole and only the silence of moon surrounded us.

'What does he mean, you lose?' I asked. 'He thought I was trying to trick him.'

'Weren't you?'

'No.'

From the corner of my golden goggles I saw a disc-shaped light approaching noiselessly. The craft hovered above and to the side of ours. A shaft of light stretched out from the underside and hit the ground directly below it. Rachel descended down through the light, suspended on her back, her arms and legs sprawled. She wasn't wearing any protective suit.

My mother walked into the light and caught Rachel's body in her arms. With the second ship's light still upon her, light from our own ship stretched down and moved across the surface of the moon towards her, until the two lights met and my mother and Rachel were at their intersection. The first light fell away and the ship flew off the way it had come. My mother and Rachel were carried up to our ship and it darted into the black sky, hovered for a moment as a luminous speck in the distance, then shot across the sky and away from my view. I stood alone in the crater on the moon.

Chapter 47

Desolation Rock

I stared at the darkness above the crater. I waited for my mother's ship to return. She did not come back. I was afraid. I stared and stared at the blackness and I hoped she would return before it was too late for the plan she had to be put into action, but the darkness remained constant and undisturbed. She did not come back.

I walked away from where the red eye had emerged and I tried to fly out of the crater but I could not. I already knew I would not be able to fly on the moon, but I feared that I had also lost all of the magic I'd learnt on Earth. I returned to the wall of the crater and tried to climb out, but the slope worked against me and the diminished gravity did nothing to propel me to freedom.

Any time, I thought, the hole in the face of the crater's wall would open and the eye would return. Or another spaceship would arrive above the crater and take me to him, to Titus Titus, who had won me in a trade for another life. But the walls of the crater did not open and a spaceship did not come.

Fear gave way to boredom.

I kicked at the grey ground to watch the sand rise and fall slower than sand would rise and fall on Earth. It was as if I was watching a movie in slow motion through the lens of my suit. My eyes settled on a little rock that looked like a tiny degraded pyramid. I bent to pick up the rock and look under it for a barcode, knowing there wouldn't be one. I shook my head thinking of the people on Earth who still held firm that man had never been to the moon and America had filmed the entire Apollo mission on Earth. If only they could see me now.

I took a single step forward and said out loud, 'One small step for man. One giant leap for mankind.' I tried to do Michael Jackson's moonwalk. I was as bad at it on the moon as I was on Earth. I pranced around, considered the depth of the crater over and over again, and inspected every bit of its wall for a way out.

Hours went by and my grey rocky surroundings remained constant. The length and depth of my thoughts were the only evidence of the passing of time. Fear returned and dissolved over and over again. My heart exhausted its strength to beat fast. My spirit tired of its fear.

Loneliness replaced everything. Loneliness on the moon was different and strange. I longed for the enemy's ship that I had feared would come. I longed for the red eye, for its voice that at least sounded human. It didn't matter whose voice it was. I was alone on the moon. I did not know whether I had been betrayed or sacrificed. I did not know what fate awaited me. I did not know anything. Any trace of another life would have satisfied a need I had never confronted before. You are not human without another human to relate to.

The hours passed. I explored every inch of the crater until I was bored of seeing the same rocks again. I sat on the lunar surface that was hard beneath its soft layer of dust, and I thought of the plight of a prisoner punished with solitary confinement, without a clock to tell the time, or a changing sky to guess it by. In the end, the absolute constancy of my predicament, the perfect uniformity of my situation, not being able to watch the hands of a watch or the neon digital count-up of time ticking away, was what got me. I had been left alone on the moon, in a crater indistinguishable from any other. Back on Earth, people would look up at the night sky and see the silvery luminance of the distant moon, but they would not suspect that there was a human being like them sitting along in a hole, abandoned and stranded.

What if this was my end? What if Titus Titus never came to take me, and my mother never returned to save me? What if I died in the crater and my human body was reduced to bones under the strange fabric of my spacesuit? What if this was the plan all along? What if it was not a plan but a deception? What if this was a thing that could happen to anyone, and some saw the snare and avoided it while some fell for it? What if only I had fallen for it?

Perhaps there were infinite craters on infinite moons, graveyards to infinite fools like me who had thought they could fly, that their mothers could slay dragons, and that they were something special?

What if hubris had lured me to a lonely, painful death? I cried in my space suit.

The hours stretched into days counted by sleeping and waking.

The days stretched into melancholy and regret. Sadness and fear, through hunger and thirst, multiplied. Absolute fear became absolute madness.

Out of the corner of my lens I would see a rock shift upon the lunar surface. When I turned to catch its intent, its motion would have ended and with not a particle of dust falling in low gravity. In the cocoon of my spacesuit I would hear voices whispering, but as soon as I listened to what they said they would stop. I would continue to listen, but they wouldn't talk again until I had stopped paying attention to them. I screamed. I cried. I swore. I laughed. I was going mad, but at least I still knew it.

Then, at the apex of my lonesome sorrow, death arrived in the failing of the breathing apparatus embedded somewhere in the essence of my spacesuit. I remembered what my mother had said, that the suit afforded me forty days of support, and I felt a burst of elation. In that total, absolute, unyielding, and relentless wilderness, any event would have made a difference. I approached my death with the excitement of discovery for, at last, I knew how many days had passed.

Chapter 48

Through an Infant's Eyes

'Traveller, your life support system will soon expire. If you have another one, you must go to a safe place and change into it now. This one will expire by the time I count to one thousand, by which time you will have died. If you do not wish to hear me counting, you may say stop at any time. One, two, three, four, five... '

The female voice of the suit was the first voice I'd heard since I'd been abandoned on the moon. It was as passionless and impersonal as a pre-recorded message could be, yet listening to it count up to my death was the most soothing thing I had ever experienced. It was the voice of another human. It was sweet and it was beautiful, and in it I heard the voices of all the people I had ever known.

And thus began my long, drawn out flashback of a life that had been as unremarkable as it had been under-whelming until a few days ago when magic came to seek me.

As the oxygen depleted, my mind faded and I could no longer attach names to the faces being served up in my memory. A woman I had thought was my nanny became just another person with hazy features floundering in a region of my brain where images flattened like two-dimensional pictures and floated away from me as I sailed headfirst towards a light that kept getting brighter.

My body rose gently into the light. I wasn't breathing but I wasn't suffocating. I knew I was dead, or close to death. Titus Titus bent over me and held my hand. He pulled me up out of my spacesuit and we floated together up into a viewing chamber; a large dome the size of a little house. In the gigantic ship we flew over the empty redness of Mars. We sailed along with the rocky rings of Saturn.

We flew far out until the entire mass of our solar system was framed within our dome. We travelled through galaxies. I witnessed the magnificence of a black hole. I watched two suns orbiting one another. We went beyond the stars and I saw things that the human mind cannot comprehend and human words cannot describe.

We dropped into the orbit of a moonless planet. It was yellow and pink, and its weather was green. We left that world for another not far away, where we hovered above trees whose roots clung to the flowing gas that was the ground, and whose black crystal leaves moved and morphed with a current of energy that blew their diamond seeds around. We approached twin planets revolving around each other in a galactic tango. We flew close to the one whose surface was like Earth's, with firm ground and flora growing from it. Beings like dinosaurs inhabited the grassy valleys, humanoids with clubs and leaves to cover their bodies waved their weapons and threw stones at us. We flew to the opposite world, visible from the first as a large blue moon. Our ship cruised above the skyscrapers there, and the people, much like us, waved from the windows of their flying crafts that sailed just a little way below ours.

We left the two worlds and sailed through their sun. The white, flowing plasma washed over our ship like liquid marble.

We flew past countless galaxies and the worlds within them, and we came to a place that was black and empty, and the blackness pulsated. We witnessed the birth of a star. We watched the death of a world.

We travelled even further out. The dark void we sailed into became a blue sky. We sailed on and the blue changed to purple and then to green. We sailed further and the dome above us was as woven fabric, with fibres as large as my arm. We sailed further and the sky was cloth. We sailed even further and the cloth was white with blue stripes. We sailed even further and the white and blue stripes became a bib around an infant's neck. The child was red. Its features were like ours, but blue flame clung to his head where we had hair. My heart staggered at the thought of the size of this alien infant being, if we had come from galaxies within galaxies within an atom within a fibre of its bib.

Titus Titus looked at me. He was neither smiling nor glowering. I had seen what he wanted me to see and that was enough for him and for me. I understood why he had brought me there.

Chapter 49

To Die Breathing

'Six hundred and sixty seven, six hundred and sixty eight...' The female voice of my suit continued counting.

I opened my eyes. I was being carried. I blinked to clear my failing sight. My legs were in the clutches of hooded people in long black cloaks each side of me. Two more held my hands. Ahead, another two walked, their long cloaks softly billowing in the stillness of the moon.

I closed my eyes and let the voice of my suit carry me away.

I gasped as I awoke. I sat up and gulped deep breaths. Hands held me back from sitting up. I was captive, but I was alive. I was breathing again and I wasn't in the suit. I was naked. My bare skin was on a hard, elevated surface. The mist cleared from my eyes and I looked round me. The hooded people who had carried me from the crater held up glowing rocks whose green luminescence was all the light there was.

I continued filling my lungs with gulp after gulp of air – almost running out of oxygen had made me greedy for the stuff. I seemed to be in a cave but I couldn't see how high it was, or how wide. There were at least one hundred hooded people around me, their bodies hidden beneath their sackcloths. They were all looking at me. The banished magicians my mother talked about. Any time now their leader would come to claim the prize that he had hauled in. Perhaps he was already there, snarling at me beneath one of the black hoods.

At my feet, one of them raised a hand from within the depths of their black cloak and drew away their hood. In the glow of the green light I saw that it was a woman. Her thinning hair was white or blonde, and it reflected the green light. Her cheekbones were pronounced under her stretched pale skin. She was starving or sick, and her bulging eyes looked sad.

'Are you Mr Magic?' she said.

'Who are you?' I asked as I sat up.

'My name is Galigangangah. You should know. You should know who I am. You are Mr Magic. You are, aren't you?'

'Where am I?'

'Have you come to save us?'

'Where is he?'

'Who?'

'Titus Titus. Where am I?'

'You don't know where you are?'

Of course I knew. I was on the moon. But when I woke up and I wasn't dead, and I knew that the place I was in was not a kind of afterlife, I expected to be the prisoner of the magicians on the moon. Instead I had been rescued by prisoners who expected me to rescue them. And they knew my name. Or at least, Mr Magic's name.

'Galigangah,' I said. 'Galigangangah.'

'Galigangangah, I was almost dead in a crater before you rescued me.'

'You cannot die.'

'I assure you, I was dying. I was almost dead.'

'No. You have been on the surface for one hundred days without oxygen and you are still alive. Nobody who is human can survive that long.'

'I was only there for forty days.'

'No. You were there for one hundred days. Itohan told us where to find you.'

'Itohan? My mother?'

'We don't know who she is. She brings us medicine. She told us you had come to the moon.'

'Galigangangah, I want to answer all your questions, but first you must answer mine. Who are you and where am I?'

Galigangangah spoke to the rest of them.

'He is tired. He needs to rest.'

She repeated, I assumed, the same thing in ten different languages that I counted by the number of sentences. I had never heard any of them but different sections of the crowd responded with 'ohs' and 'ahs', a universal sound of understanding.

She said something else that was shorter that she didn't first say in English. Murmuring spread through the cave.

Galigangangah looked at me. 'You need to rest. When you feel better, you will tell us what to do.'

'Were you also in the crater? Did you bring me here? No. They did.'

Galigangangah pointed at the people by my sides. The cloaks fell off their bodies, three of them on either side of me. They were not human. They were a reddish brown. Their skin looked like the texture of an elephant's, even though their bodies looked more like snakes. Their heads were tapered at the end of long necks like a dinosaur. At the end of the neck, which was half their height, the rest of their bodies split into two equal parts, each the same size as their neck. Their 'legs' rested on the floor at right angles and continued on the ground as if they were large mutant pythons raised on their bellies. They were like upside down Ys curved at the tips. Strange as the otherworldly beings' appearance was, however, I was not afraid, and indeed they ought to have been frightful to any human. But only recently I had travelled galaxies upon galaxies and marvelled at the indescribable beings that populate the planets therein, even the gigantic planets construct-ed from scratch by the strange beings who created such artificial planets to live upon. Dream though it was, I had seen it all.

Chapter 50

Strange Letter G

My hallucinations, as I lay dying on the moon, had taught me something about myself that I would never have known had my brain cells not reached the terminal frenzied firings of the final stages before death. Who I was, or who people thought I was, was nothing. It was infinitesimally insignificant. Whatever I did or did not do meant nothing. Could I save these people? It did not matter. Was I still on the moon? That didn't matter either. Would they ever be saved? That, also, meant nothing. They wanted Mr Magic. I would be who they wanted me to be. It meant nothing either way.

'I do not need to rest,' I said. 'How many of you are here?'

'We don't know. There are others who have escaped.'

'Are we on the beautiful side of the moon?'

'Yes. Underneath their city.'

'They brought you here?'

'They brought all of us here.'

'How long have you been here?'

'Since I was eighteen. I was taken from a play. I was alone backstage waiting to come on. My parents were in the audience. I have been here for twelve years.'

She used to be an actress.

Another woman took her hood off. She was black. Her grey dreadlocks extended to the ground. 'They took me on my wedding day,' she said.

All around, they uncovered their heads, or shed their cloaks. There were so many different beings.

'I was playing hide and seek with my twin sister,' another human said. 'I hid in a cupboard under the stairs. They took me from there. I was sleeping when they took me.'

'I was in the bathtub.'

'I was driving to the hospital in a blizzard. I gave birth to her in the car. They took both of us.'

'I was robbing a bank with my girlfriend. I went into the safe. They took me from there.'

'I was saying confession when they took me.'

'My brother told me to come and see a light outside the house.

They took me then.'

'My father was pushing me on a swing. I fell into a well.'

'I had just climbed into my neighbour's tree house. I was praying.'

They took turns telling me how they had been stolen from their lives. It seemed important to them to tell me, so I listened.

There was not one male amongst the different beings. I did not ask why. They expected me to know.

'What about them?' I asked about the reptile beings.

'We don't know where they are from,' Galigangangah said, 'but they were also taken.'

'Do they talk?'

'No. But they draw and they write. And they can understand us.'

One of them lowered her head to me. Her eyelids blinked over a completely black eye. She motioned with her head for me to follow. She turned and began to move as if walking, one 'leg' going before the other, only the 'legs' didn't actually lift from the ground. The others made way for her. I lowered my feet to the ground. They sank into soft sand. I followed the being to the end of the cave.

The rock face was covered in drawings and symbols scratched onto it. She turned her head to me, then swivelled it around to point at an image.

Scratched onto the rock was a triangle with its right side bent into itself like the letter G. It meant nothing to me.

'We have not been able to decipher their language but we know they were here before us. Those had been written before we got here,' Galigangangah said.

Another of the beings walked up to the wall. Looking at me, she raised the end of one of her legs and drew beneath the image using a small rock.

She looked at me all the time, drawing with her back to the rock face she drew upon. Above the symbol, she drew a saucer. She drew two parallel lines coming out of the saucer and ending on either sides of the triangle. She moved her writing rock to lines of tiny symbols that had been etched onto the rock. I moved closer to see. She pointed the rock at a particular symbol. It was the strange G. She pointed to another line and there again was the rectangular G.

All through the lines, in several places, the strange G appeared and I understood. The symbols were not letters, they were words. Their language had a symbol for every word and I was the rectangular G. I was their Mr Magic as well.

Chapter 51

Space Robot

I turned to the people, the humans and the others. They were every age. They were all thin and they all wore an expression of hopelessness on their faces, even as they looked at the one they had all hoped for.

'Why didn't Itohan save you?' I asked Galigangangah.

'If they find out she comes here, and she takes any one of us, they will take a hundred more for the one she rescues. She told us you will save all of us.'

'You said you escaped. How?'

'There are tunnels. Others before us dug them. Every time they discover a tunnel, they fill it up. We dig new ones all the time so others can escape.'

'What do they do to you?'

'Nothing. They return some, the rest they keep. They examine us. They take samples from us. They inject things into us. They give us coins and they take them back. When they are done, they leave us.'

'Coins? What do they want you to do with the coins? Nothing. They just watch us.'

'Where exactly do they keep you?'

'Nowhere. They just leave us.'

'They just leave you to wander about?'

'They just leave us. We gather together and when we find the tunnels we escape.'

I looked at them. They were all looking at me. I knew why they had been taken.

'Listen, everyone. They took you because they are afraid of you.

'You are as powerful as they are. You can do everything they can do. Even if you don't know it, they do. They kept you because they are afraid to harm you. They know that the instant they try, you will react with the power that is in your instinct.

'I have come to save you. I know you expected something else. An army with weapons, perhaps. But I have my army here. You are my army and we are our own weapons. We will return to the surface and you will return to your homes in their ships. We will defeat them, but you must believe you can. You are like them.'

Galigangangah finished interpreting my words and they all stood silently looking at me.

Galigangangah spoke to me. 'What do you mean when you say we are like them?'

'You are like them. I am like them. We are all like them.'

'The robots?'

'Robots?'

'Yes. Robots. They are all robots.'

Chapter 52

Doubting Women

When in doubt, don't show it. My line manager used to say so.

Robots on the moon made more sense than a colony of magicians in lunar exile, but Titus Titus was no robot and neither were his goons, at least not the ones I met and dealt with back on Earth. But these women had been kidnapped by robots, and as far as they knew, only the robots lived on the so-called beautiful side of the moon. Robots and magic and flying saucers and aliens simply didn't seem to belong together. Robots, especially, threw me. But if I was in doubt, I'd better not show it.

'Is your name Mr Magic or not?' Galigangangah asked.

'Yeah. Sure. Absolutely. That is my name. Mr Magic. And I have come to take you all back to your homes.'

'Do you know what the robots want from us? Why they took us?'

I could not look her in the eye and lie. It would also have made it worse if I started talking about magic and tattoos that turned to dragons and Titus Titus and the Great Schism.

'I don't know,' I said. I waited for dismay.

303

'Do you work for the space alliance?'

'The space alliance?'

'Yes. The space alliance. Itohan works for the space alliance.'

'Oh. Yeah. The space alliance. Yes. I work for them. I mean, I'm from the space alliance. Yes. I'm Mr Magic of the space alliance. That's me.'

'Who are you?'

'I told you. Mr Magic. Of the space alliance. And I've come to...'

'To take us all back to our homes. Yes, we've heard you say so. How are you going to get us back home if you didn't know about the robots and if you don't have a ship.'

'We will use their ships.'

'How many ships do they have?'

'I don't know.'

'Can you fly their ships?'

'No. Not yet.'

'Do you know where they keep them?'

'No.'

'Have you ever been to the moon before?'

'No.'

'How exactly are you going to save us?'

'I don't know, Galigangangah. I really don't know. But I know I can save you. This was my mother's plan all along. I am meant to be here. I am meant to save you. This is why she left me on the moon. To save you. You have to trust me.'

'Why should I trust you?'

'Because I am Mr Magic and Itohan told you I would rescue you.'

'Maybe you're not the one. How did you get to the moon? Where is your ship?'

'My ship? I did not need one.'

'How did you get here?'

'It's not how I got here that matters. What matters is that I am here now. I have to get to the surface and I need someone to show me the way. Who can take me to the surface?'

She stared at me.

'Who can take me to the surface?'

Her silence pulsated with anger and despair. She turned to the rest, and with a raised voice she said: 'He wants to know who can take him to the surface?' Then she repeated it in the different languages and when she was done she faced me and the silence in the cave was unnerving. I knew that they knew that there was something wrong. They sensed that I wasn't the saviour they'd expected, that I was not going to save them. It was a real possibility that at any time they could turn on me and return me to the crater from which they'd rescued me.

'I will take you,' Galigangangah said. She turned to the rest of them and said, 'I will take him to the surface,' then she interpreted it in their various languages.

'Thank you,' I said.

'Don't thank me,' she said. 'I just want to get rid of

you.'

Galigangangah gave me one of the black cloaks they wore. It smelt sweet, like potpourri, and it was light and soft against the skin. I had been bare before them all the while, but only when they gave me something to cover myself did I truly feel naked.

Galigangangah and I began the journey back to the surface through a narrow tunnel behind a boulder, which they rolled away. She was in front and she held one of the glowing stones so we could see where we were going as we crawled on our bellies, an exercise that consumed considerably less effort than if we'd been on Earth. It hit me then that in the cave we had walked as if we were on Earth. I wanted to ask her how this was possible but I knew that doing so would only further expose my lack of knowledge, which in her mind made me a dangerous imposter.

'Galigangangah,' I said, 'can I ask you something?'

She did not stop and she did not respond. But at least she had not said no.

'You said you wanted to get rid of me,' I said. 'What did you mean by that?'

'I meant I want to get rid of you. I will take you to the surface but you must not come back.'

'Why?'

'We are all women, all of us, even the reds that rescued you.'

'Reds. That's what you call them?'

'Do you know what they are?'

306

'No. How do you know they are female?'

'Women know other women.'

'Ok. What does that have to do with wanting to get rid of me?'

'None of us has seen a man since we were taken. If you have not come to rescue us, I don't want you around us.'

'Oh. Ok. I get it.'

We continued in silence. We were climbing all the time in a spiralling gentle slope that seemed to go on and on. We must have been climbing for an hour, and even though the ascent required little effort, my arms were getting tired and my tummy had sounded off its second rumble.

'What do you eat?' I said.

'There are rocks full of minerals.'

'You eat rocks?'

'Plants don't grow on the moon.'

'And you are able to survive on this?'

She stopped for the first time since we left. Perhaps she had some edible rocks on her.

'I'm good for now,' I said.

'Sh. Did you hear that?'

'Hear what?'

'That.'

'No. Oh. That's my tummy.'

'Oh. Ok. We are close. We haven't finished digging this one so you'll have to dig your way through.'

'This is not the tunnel you escaped through?'

307

'No. We filled up the one we used with rocks, so that we won't be found. We were digging this one for others, just like other people dug the one we used, but now we must fill this one up and start all over again.'

She plastered herself to the wall of the tunnel to let me pass. I did not much like her plan but I squeezed past her all the same. Our bodies brushed against one another and I felt just how emaciated she was. She held my arm to stop me when we were aligned flush against each other.

'I don't know who you are,' she said, 'and I don't know why Itohan told us to get you. But if you come back, I will crack your skull on a rock.'

She began to crawl backwards down the tunnel. She took her light with her and I watched her green illuminated features fading away.

Chapter 53

The Beautiful Side Of The Moon

I was alone, underground, in a tight tunnel on the moon. There was no light, so I could not see anything. Ahead of me was a wall of rocks that only yielded trickles of sand to my fingers; behind was death. It wasn't long before my mind began to compare my current situation to that of someone unlucky enough – or the victim of treachery vile enough – to be buried alive. What if they closed the tunnel behind me? What if I dig and dig and never make it to the surface? What if this was how Galigangangah planned to get rid of me, by entombing me in an anonymous hole beneath the lunar surface, my name, my life, all I had done and all that I was, forever lost, forever inconsequential, forever forgotten.

Inevitable panic arrived with a quickening of my heartbeat. I dug with my hands till my nails cracked and my fingers bled. I scraped the loose sand and injured myself on the rocks. I pushed what I managed to free down past me into the tunnel. Galigangangah said the surface was close; if that was not a lie, did she mean close in distance, or close in the time it would take me to dig my way through? At the rate I was progressing, (in my estimation I was tunnelling through one foot an hour), it would take me six hours to dig my own length, but exactly how many feet, or metres, or miles to the surface was it?

What if she had led me to the wrong side of the moon, to where the air was poison to my human lungs? I stopped digging. I hotly despised my own brain for serving up all the possible traps I could be digging myself into. For once in my life, I understood the oft-quoted adage that ignorance is bliss. When I continued digging again, it was slowly and with trepidation, because the next handful of sand and rock I dislodged could bring my own death tumbling down with it.

A few fistfuls of moon substance later and my fingers stretched into open air. I panicked and withdrew my hand in a flash, my fingers tingling with fear of the danger they might have been exposed to. A ray of light stretched into the hole I had made. I held my breath and retreated the few inches I could move in the tight space. When my lungs were bursting, and my skin was not melting from poisonous gas, and my eyeballs were not peppered or burning, I exhaled, still fearful that the next breath I took would be my last. When my lungs were emptied of life-sustaining oxygen, I took a tiny exploratory breath. The air was good to breathe. I made the hole just large enough to get a better look. Outside was brilliant as day. I was looking up at the sky, and from my limited point of view I could tell that very high above me there was a glass dome, beyond which the blackness of space prevailed. In the dome there was light, but I could not yet see where from. I listened for sounds. There were none. I considered waiting till night to make my exit, then I remembered there was no night and day on the moon, only constant light and constant darkness, depending on the side.

I listened. I dug in intervals. When I had made a hole large enough to fit through, I waited in case the people or robots I had not seen or heard were waiting for me outside the tunnel.

I inched my head out, ready to retreat into the tunnel in an instant, like a tortoise into its shell, at the slightest hint of danger. There was nothing around me save for rocks embedded in dusty sand. The dome above was so immense that I could not see where it touched the ground. It was as high as the sky was far from the Earth's surface.

I climbed out and shook the dust off my cloak. Standing upright I saw beyond the boulders encircling me. I saw the land of the robots.

Tall windowless steel structures rose from the ground in clusters. Between them, white shimmering roads weaved in and out.

I saw the robots too. I was at the edge of town and they were busy constructing a new tower of steel and laying the road around it. They worked with torches and laser cutters. They were every shape of robot I had ever seen, and a few I had never imagined or would never have imagined. They were built for the purpose they served, so the one welding plates of steel together was an upright cylinder on tractor wheels and had four arms, two to hold things together in place and two that were welding heads.

There were humanoid ones too. They appeared to supervise the work. Between the workers, tiny machines flitted about getting in the way. They were after discarded scraps of building material. The other robots shooed them away with their chainsaw hands and laser tails.

It was indeed a city of robots. I did not see any abducted humans or magicians. But what need would robots have for houses?

I shook the remaining dust off my cloak and started walking towards them.

Chapter 54

Silhouettes of Fire

Like someone walking towards a pack of wild animals, I approached the robots with caution. As I got closer, I began to differentiate the various sounds they caused; the clanks of their feet on concrete, the steady grind of their tractor wheels upon the tarmac they were laying, the rhythmic, perfect cadence of the bangs of their hammers, the rotor scream of their electric screwdrivers. But they made no sounds themselves – no machine noises or clunks or whirling emitted from their metallic bodies. Their silence made them seem more real, almost alive, in a way. They also moved with the fluidity and natural grace of animals. They were the most advanced robots I'd ever seen, in real life or in the movies. They seemed organic.

I walked slowly into their midst. I kept my arms steady by my sides. I stopped and stood still when I was deep amongst them. They just carried on with their work. To them, I was simply another obstacle to navigate around. The tiny playful ones gathered at my feet – they were all sorts of shapes. Some had many 'eyes', lenses through which they looked at me, some had two, and some had only one. Those who had necks, or the robot equivalent, bent them from side to side and studied me from different angles. I stayed perfectly still and waited for the bigger ones to take notice of me.

The little robots, like little children, got bored with the unresponsive thing and they moved on, but I remained unchallenged by the workers. Perhaps watching them seemingly communicating and interacting, like labourers and their foremen on Earth, had made me erroneously assume I'd found artificial intelligence on the moon. Perhaps if I said to these robots, 'I come in peace', or 'Take me to your leader,' they would neither understand nor react to the joke.

They could not serve my purpose, so I continued on my way along the white shimmering road they were building, hoping to find the one I was looking for. I encountered many more robots and none of them paid me any attention. They were mindless worker beings, programmed to build houses and streets and no more. I was getting dismayed. I suspected that the strength of my conviction, which gave me a confidence that I had not examined for fear of jinxing it, would begin to waver as I had more and more time to question my own courage.

The further I walked along the road that was wide but devoid of vehicles, past buildings that were tall but windowless, the more I began to wonder if it wasn't just a city of robots. I passed side roads that didn't look interesting, then I came to a wide open junction the size of a football field. There the roads split into three, all equally spaced, and the buildings were much taller, like the tallest skyscrapers on Earth. But the tall buildings were still just steel monoliths that had no doors or windows or balconies or anything. I felt I had come to the middle of town, but all around me the only life was the robots cleaning, sweeping, welding, and building. And they were not even alive.

I stood and looked around me, at the busy machines and the lifeless city. Then suddenly they all stopped. The sound of a chainsaw was last to die. The silence was absolute. I looked about me for what had made them stop. It was then that I noticed their metal heads were turned to me and their glass eyes were staring at me. It was as if a pride of lions had suddenly noticed the gazelle that had wandered into their midst. They outnumbered me thousands to one. I was the gazelle about to be devoured.

Together, they began to close in on me. From all directions they approached, their gaze never leaving me.

I tried, but I could not read the intentions of the machines. But their slow deliberate progress towards me wasn't friendly.

The grinding plate at the end of the single hand of a robot on wheels began to spin. One by one all their tools began to switch back on. The one with chainsaws for arms started revving its cutting chain with jagged diamond teeth. Blue flame jetted from the hands of a welder robot. One with a long arm that lacked an elbow and ended in the bulbous head of a large sledgehammer dragged its heavy hammer along the ground, scratching a trail behind it.

By now, they were less than a few metres from me. I

was within easy reach of their tools.

I put up my hand and I said, 'Wait.'

They stopped, but their weapons continued flaming and spinning.

I felt it in me. It was like a swelling in my chest. It was a most powerful emotion. Its intensity made my eyes burn. I wanted to cry, I wanted to scream. My heart smiled. My excitement was uncontainable. My entire body tingled from my most unbelievable discovery.

I raised my other hand and brought my palms together.

With savage ferocity, the robots turned on one another. They sawed each other's arms off. They torched each other's bodies, they twisted steel heads till they popped out, drilled into metallic chests, and ripped out wiring.

All around, the sound of brutal mechanical warfare wheezed and scraped and screeched. Even the little ones were not spared as they were trampled and flattened in the melee. Then the ground shook in time with a heavy thud in distance. A moment passed and the ground shook again with another thud. Something huge was approaching. I waited for it.

A gigantic metal robot stepped into view between two rows of skyscrapers on one of the three roads leading away from where I stood, and the ground shook heavily under its footsteps. It was at least five storeys high. Its metallic body was featureless, even its hands lacked fingers – there was just a thumb and a palm. It marched on. It kicked the warring robots out of its path or simply stamped them beneath its feet. At the foot of the junction it stopped, its blank face staring at me, then the ground shook again with another heavy thud. Two more giant robots marched out from the other roads. Like the first, they too stopped and stared, all of them equidistant from me. They had me boxed in.

I waved my hand at the first one but its mechanical being did not respond to my command. I tried another one, then the one behind me, but all of them were immune to my will.

Then I noticed something about the battle of the smaller robots. The way they waged war with ingenious savagery suggested that they indeed had their own minds – minds that were able to imagine such creative destructiveness, just like the minds of the humans who had made them. But not so with the colossal beings that had just arrived. They, unlike the smaller robots, were true mindless puppets controlled by others whose minds I could not access.

The first of the giants suddenly took on an orange glow all over the front of its body, like metal heating up, until it was fiery red. This burning lump of metal split away from the body of the great robot and ran towards me, leaving robots melting in the burning footsteps it left behind. The other two robots also shed fiery clones of themselves, and the freed masses of fire were running towards me too.

There was only one thing left for me to do. I looked up to the dome of glass above me and I flew straight up, leaving the silhouettes of fire to run into each other. I looked down even as I braced for the huge explosion as they crashed into one another, but rather than be destroyed in a ball of fire as I'd hoped, they merged into one, and a larger burning beast was born, three times as big as the original ones. Its body of fire burned with three times the intensity. It stretched its hands up towards me where I hovered just beneath the highest point of the dome. It rose from the ground and flew towards me, shedding tongues of flame behind it.

Chapter 55

Cool Moon Fire

The heat from the fiery beast warmed me up quickly as it flew straight at me. In no time it would reach me and incinerate me in the flaming hands stretched out in front of it for just that purpose. I considered breaking through the dome above me, but that would make the air unbreathable for the abductees hidden in the caves below, and I wasn't sure I could survive in space myself, or continue to fly for that matter. The beast was so big there was no way I could outfly it. Even if we played a game of dodge across the inner circumference of the dome, it was only a matter of time before it held me in its grip of fire.

It was really close. The heat radiating from it was unbearable and I could not look directly at the glare of its body.

I flew headfirst, flat against the curve of the dome. Below, the beast changed directions to follow me, shedding more flame as it turned. By the intensity of the heat, I judged when I was far enough from it, then I let myself fall. I passed the burning mass on my way down. It was already changing its direction. The three giant robots were still standing in place, their heads turned up to me. In rapid succession their bodies glowed and they shed flaming copies of themselves over and over again. Each of the burning silhouettes ran straight ahead as they were created, and merged in the middle. The beast that had been after me landed in the burning mass beneath us and immediately became several times bigger. The robots kept emitting more and more copies and the beast of fire kept growing bigger and brighter.

I landed on the flat top of a steel building. I shielded my face with my arm, to protect my eyes from the brilliance of the monster that was now as tall as the skyscrapers. The beast burnt with such intensity that a wind of scorching heat blew out from it. The edges of my cloak began to smoulder, tiny embers blew away from it. The steel beneath my bare feet became too hot to stand on. The beast continued to grow.

Soon its head would reach the top of the dome.

I flew away towards the edge of town. With strides that spanned entire blocks, the fire monster followed me. My cloak began to smoke all over as it disintegrated around me in tiny sparks. The hair on my exposed legs curled from the heat and reduced to ashes. The soles of my feet began to blister.

Ahead, the boulders shone brightly and the ground reflected the light of the beast. I flew over a great crater several miles wide and landed in its centre. My cloak had completely burnt off me. As the giant approached, the shadow of the crater swept over me. The beast jumped into the crater with one leap. It straightened itself and continued to march towards me.

I fell to one knee and spread my fingers into the sand. The beast stood over me. My head, my back and my neck, exposed to it, began to flame.

My fingers became wet, then my knee, then my legs, then the water rose like a wave up from the ground and fully submerged me. The giant turned to run away but the water rose to its feet and the flame sizzled away. The water continued to rise. Its surface bubbled and steamed as it ate the beast. With one final hiss, the monster was totally extinguished.

I rose to the surface of the water. Where moments before there had been a crater, a lake now shimmered, calm and clear. I walked on the surface of the water to the shore. There, robots had gathered to watch.

Behind them the three tall ones stood in a row. As I stepped onto the land, the robots parted. I walked towards the three giants. I felt they still had some fight in them.

One by one the giants charged. They formed a straight line as they came for me.

I stopped and spread out my arms. Blue flame formed over the front of my body. It felt as cool as a Harmattan breeze blowing across my face. The blue fire stepped away from my body, walked towards the approaching robots and inflated in size until it was as large as them. The first robot ran through the body of fire and stepped out through its back. It lifted its foot to take one more stride but its steel body melted to the ground. The next robot tried to stop, digging its feet into the soil, but it continued sliding forward. The blue giant punched a hole through the centre of its chest. The robot slumped onto its slayer's body and huge drops of molten steel fell from its head, its shoulders, and its chest.

The third robot managed to stop. It watched the second robot melt down to its waist before the rest of it toppled over, and it turned round and ran. The blue giant leapt up. With one bound it sailed over the fleeing robot and landed in front it. The robot turned to run the other way but the burning giant flew towards it, caught up with it and wrapped its arms around it from behind. The fleeing robot threw its hands up as it melted in the fiery embrace.

The blue giant walked up to me and stood in front of me. Its beam on my face was cool and comforting. The worker robots stood far from us and watched. The giant's body of brilliant blue fire broke into a million tiny sparks that floated away and rose upwards as they died. Behind it, where it had stood, a dozen figures dressed in black floated forward just above the ground. The magicians. Titus Titus floated in front of them. As I watched, more of them floated forward. Together they formed a chain over a hundred magicians wide, and behind them several hundreds more floated out to join the army.

The robots backed away from me, and the magicians sailed forwards.

Chapter 56

The Moon Revisited

The magicians formed a large circle around me. They were all ages, all colours, all shapes, and all sizes. They were men and women, boys and girls. That I was naked and they were clothed made me uncomfortable, but I did not feel vulnerable. I was not afraid of them.

Titus Titus floated forward and stopped halfway to me. His face did not have its smirk. His tattoos did not move on his skin. His presence did not oppress my spirit. I was no longer afraid of him and he knew it.

We looked into each other's eyes. Not a sound could be heard for miles on the moon. Robots and magicians stayed perfectly still, the former standing, the latter floating, all watching and waiting.

'You cannot be here,' Titus Titus said. 'You made your choice. You are one of them. The truce is broken. You have broken the truce.'

He turned to the magicians. 'The truce is broken.' He turned to announce the news to another section on his fellows. 'The truce is broken.'

A murmur grew and spread amongst the magicians, then suddenly there was a loud noise like the continuous blast of a horn. The noise was so loud that it made the rocks vibrate and the sand leap from the ground, and its resonance reached inside my body and shook me to the core. It was coming from everywhere, from all directions, and it filled me with pain.

Space ships slid in sideways through a slit in the middle of the dome and descended. They floated above the magicians. Hundreds flew in from the darkness of space. They lined up over the magicians. They let down beams of light that carried the magicians up to their ships, then the ships slid out of the dome through the slit at the top from where they had entered and vanished into the dark vastness of space.

In the end, only Titus Titus and I were left facing each other, and his own ship rotated in position above his head.

He spoke to me but I couldn't hear him over the terrible noise. The sound had made me fall to my knees and my hands were pressed so hard against my ears that it felt like I was crushing my own skull.

He wanted me to hear what he said and he repeated it again. In agony I concentrated on his lips as he spoke. He said, 'It is your fault.'

A beam of light poured out of his ship and sucked him up.

His ship slipped out through the slit in the dome and the glass closed up, and after that the sound died away.

I got to my feet. I was alone on the surface of the moon. Even the robots had fled. The magicians had deserted their place of exile. Titus Titus had fled with them.

But what he said stayed with me: 'It is your fault.'

Even though his face had lost its power to scare me, something in his words was terribly unsettling and I knew I should be worried.

It was my fault. What was my fault?

I thought of the women underground. Had they heard the terrible noise too? I had to return to them. I had to let them know it was safe to come out now. I also had to find all the other caves where all the other people were hiding. But I had no ships with which to return them to their homes.

Titus Titus said it was my fault. What was my fault?

The robots came out from the places they had gone to hide, under rocks and under the road. Some tapped on their ears. Some spun their heads around. They had also suffered from the noise. Slowly, cautiously, they gathered round me. They were the answer to my second problem. I turned on the spot. I looked each one in the eyes. Their non-human minds were mine to control. But just before I flexed that power again, I remembered how I had made them kill one another and how, in witnessing the ferocity of their battle, I had noticed that they knew what they were doing, for they could think and reason, feel pain, and be pained by death. So I spoke to them instead.

'I need your help,' I said. 'There are people like me, and some not so like me, under this ground. They were taken from their homes. They are sick and they are afraid. I wish to return them to their homes. I need ships that can

325

travel that far. I need pilots to guide those ships. Can you build me some, please?'

They were silent. They turned to one another and communicated without making a sound. A black sphere floated up from their midst. It was the red eye. It flew above them, lowered itself to the level of my head, and floated up to my face. Its metallic body opened up to reveal the red beneath and it spoke, first in the voice of Titus Titus, 'We...' Then it said a garble of unintelligible words in different voices, male and female. Then it continued in the voice of a child, 'We will return them to their homes.'

'Thank you.'

'What about us?'

'You?'

'Yes. Us. What will you do to us?'

'Do to you? Nothing. I will do nothing to you. You are free. You can do whatever you want. Whatever pleases you. Provided you stay on the moon. Is this what you want?'

'We want.'

'What?"

'We want.'

'Yes. What do you want?'

'We want.'

'I don't understand. What do you want?'

In one voice the rest of the robots spoke. They said, 'We want.'

I was surprised that they all could speak. I did not

know what they wanted, so I could not give it to them. Perhaps their synthesised intelligence had reached the limit of its ability.

'If you return the people to their homes, and you stay on this moon, and you never take any more people from any planet, then you can have what it is you want.'

The red eye blinked.

'How can we trust you?' it said. 'You promised the masters you would not return but you did.'

'I promised?'

I immediately understood. I had been to the moon before. I had been there as my father. I had made the truce with the magicians, the truce to which Titus Titus referred. The same truce I had just broken. The magicians were free to return to Earth now. Titus Titus was leading them there. That had been his plan all along. They would reveal themselves to the world, and they would display the vastness of their powers, but this time they would not be burnt at the stake. This time they were returning for revenge, and it was my fault.

Chapter 57

Alien In The Window

'I need to get to Earth right now,' I said.

The robots stared at me. I expected them to understand that I needed a spaceship immediately. The red eye hovered in front of me, just below the level of my face. It didn't blink.

'Now,' I said.

'Will you return?' the red eye said.

'No. I won't have to return because you will have returned the people to their homes. But I have to go now.'

'Ok.'

Still, not one robot moved to get me a ship. Maybe they expected me to know where they were kept. The ships that had taken the magicians away had come from beyond the dome. Perhaps even from beyond the moon. I had allowed the robots free will, and it now felt as though I was surrounded by people, rather than dumb machines. I did not want to revert to controlling them, but I had to get to Earth, pronto.

'If I do not get to Earth on time,' I said, 'they will bring more people here and I will have to come back.'

'We understand. You should go now. We hope you never return.'

They did not go to get me a ship. They just waited for me to leave. I finally understood. They had seen me come and go before, and I did not need a spaceship then.

I let myself rise gently and keep rising. Beneath me the robots closed in on the circle they had formed around me. I finally saw just how many there were. I looked at the looming curve of the dome. I took my time getting to it. I searched for the opening in the glass where the spaceships had poured in. There was no sign of it. I remembered how I had seen doors in the glasshouse open by themselves for Professor Ochuko, the very great magician of the highest level of all magicians. The dome had better open for me in the same way – me, Osaretin Osagiemwenagbon, the son of a Most Grand Magician of the First Order. And open it did, when I was still a few metres away. It was huge. What had seemed like a slit was in fact an oval-shaped opening the size of a canyon. The glass dome itself was a metre thick, and within its thickness, fist-sized veins ran, criss-crossing over one another, carrying pulses of blue light all around the dome.

Beyond the dome I saw millions and millions of stars so bright and so close together.

As I rose out of the dome, the opening sealed behind me from one end to the other like a ziplock. The further I went, the harder it became to make out the dome over the beautiful side of the moon. The dome was both a support for life and a disguise for it. In time all I could see of where I'd been was darkness, formidable and unyielding.

I had held my breath when the dome opened. I exhaled again when it closed and I discovered that I could breathe in the vacuum of space.

I did not know which way home lay. I flew away from the dark side of the moon till I saw the blue glow of Earth and I flew towards it.

I had no clothes to flap against me to hint at the speed of my flying.

The stars were so far away they moved ever so slowly against my changing position, and I did not feel the rush of wind against my face or my body, for there was no air for that. From the darkness of space, a tiny black dot crept slowly into view against the brightness of Earth. I had no idea what it could be. As I got closer, its shape became clearer and I suspected it was a satellite. When I got closer still, I realised it was far too big to be a satellite. I soon realised that I was flying towards the International Space Station. I wondered whether the astronauts had seen the spaceships, or worse, whether the magicians had also come across the human outpost and chosen it as their first port of call.

I slowed down and circled the space station. I found a hatch that opened up like a flower with huge metal petals beneath the station. Under the metal doors, glass sections were arranged to form a window for astronauts to gaze out from. Earth was its view. I flew in front of the glass. An astronaut in a blue polo shirt saw me and tumbled backwards, bumping her unprotected head against equipment on the walls of the cramped space. I turned and flew on towards Earth, hoping I wasn't too late.

Chapter 58

The Return

Several kilometres beneath me an asteroid pierced the Earth's atmosphere at an angle. A shell of orange flame enveloped the rock and stretched out behind it into a pointed tail. As the asteroid continued its fiery journey, it began to disintegrate into smaller pieces, each with its own red flaming tail. These pieces continued splitting until eventually they were just tiny sparks, none of which could compete with the furnace of re-entry.

I had survived the vacuum of space, but witnessing the light show gave me pause. I shaped my body as though I was diving, stretching myself out straight and pointing my hands and fingers in front of me, holding them together side by side over my head, which I tucked into my chest as I closed my eyes. I felt my fingers punch through the atmosphere. There was a familiar feeling of wind brushing against my skin. I opened my eyes. A beautiful jet of orange light was washing over me and I couldn't see out of the fire. I emerged into a clear blue sky over clouds that hung just beneath the tops of a belt of snow-tipped mountains. I was so glad to be back within the Earth's atmosphere again. Home suddenly had a new meaning. Earth was home, all of it, not just Lagos, or Nigeria, or

Africa. The entire globe was home. In spite of borders and religion, and war, and politics, and entry visas, and economic landscapes, the world was home to all its inhabitants equally. I was home.

I flew around the globe several times, searching for the magician's spaceships. I circled the globe again and again. I crossed day and night in minutes. I flew over cities and slums, oceans and deserts, storms and famines, wars and forests, floods and earthquakes, icebergs and tundras, pyramids and jungles, but I did not find them.

I landed in the backyard of a log cabin in the middle of a pine forest, where I had spotted clothes my size drying on a line. I flew out again in a pair of khaki cargo shorts and a black t-shirt. I couldn't afford to waste time searching for the magicians. I had to tell everybody what had happened, and warn them of what was to come.

Thankfully it was night in Nigeria, and together with a power failure, my descent from the sky onto a sidewalk in Lekki was without witness. I walked barefoot to the car wash.

I knew that Ali, the tall, slender attendant would be there. He was the keeper of the gate that led to the glasshouse through the car wash machine. And if he wasn't there, I would go through all the same. I was confident I would come out on the other side, onto the road in the desert that led to the house.

A guard at the entrance woke up and watched me walk into the compound. I noticed him looking at my bare feet.

He got up to follow me as I walked towards the machine. Ali came out of nowhere, or out of shadows – only the former now made more sense to me. He walked towards the night guard who had got to his feet and picked up his baton.

'Bro, it's ok, I know him,' Ali said, but he only managed to startle the man.

The guard held his baton tightly in both hands and alternated his attention between Ali and me.

'What are you doing here at this time?' the guard said to Ali. 'When did you return?'

'Return? I never left.'

The guard took one hand off his baton which he kept pointed at us as if it was more than a piece of wood and it could shoot bullets, and he searched under his chin for the string from which his whistle hung. He brought the whistle to his lips.

'Look at my hand,' Ali said. 'Here.' He pressed a finger into the middle of his left palm. He closed the fingers of the hand over the finger in the middle and the guard's eyes closed as well. So that was how they made me sleep.

Ali caught the man before he slumped. He lifted him as if he weighed nothing and carried him to the bench by the entrance and placed him on it, making sure he was in a comfortable position, and then he turned to me.

'Top to top,' I said. I remembered what Adesua had said to him when we used the portal.

'I know who you are,' he said. 'They are waiting for us.'

'They?'

'Yes. We are the only ones left here. The rest have gone to join the war. They told me to wait here for you.'

'War?'

'They said you broke the truce. The others have attacked and they have become more plenty and more powerful. When they defeat us, they will come here.'

'If they defeat us,' I said. 'Show me how to use this thing.'

Chapter 59

Red Rain Day

We flew out of the other side of the car wash machine into daylight on the desert road that led to the glasshouse. The beautiful blue sky above was full of clashing magicians in the distance. Beneath them, a rain of blood fell from the savage battle.

We flew side by side in heavy silence towards the war. Lifeless bodies fell from the battle in the sky.

Both sides were equally matched in magic, so they used weapons and bare hands instead of spells and magical weapons. The occasional trick was tried but the opponent would often know it as well and play the counter trick or a greater one, and occasionally a magician was turned into rock, or spontaneously combusted, or made to use their own sword on themselves, all the while trying in desperate agony to stop the limb that had been taken over.

Both sides were suffering great losses.

We got close to the carnage. I put my hand on Ali's shoulder and we stopped. He looked at me. I shook my head. He would not go further. Too many good people were already dead.

I entered the battle slowly, looking around and taking account of where the magicians on my side were. I saw

Adesua fighting with her bare hands against a man who wielded a wooden club with spikes of steel. I saw my mother thrust a sword into the belly of a man who was poised to strike her with a longer sword held over his head in both his hands.

The magician's blood dripped from the blade of my mum's weapon, which now protruded from the attacker's back. Titus Titus was gleefully swinging his sword and slitting multiple throats with each swing. I flew towards him. He saw me coming and commanded his companions to fly to me.

The magicians surrounded me, with their weapons at the ready. I floated in their midst, keeping my eyes on Titus Titus through the throng. All of a sudden they charged at me as one, and my heart was filled with great pain and sadness. I did not want to kill anyone. I stayed as I was and let them thrust their daggers and swords into my body. They attacked my body again and again and continued until they were exhausted. When they stopped to assess the damage they'd caused, I let them see that my body was still whole and their weapons had only hurt my feelings. I hoped they would give up but they attacked again. I took a sword from one of them, and in a flash I had slain them all. Pieces of my attackers fell from the sky.

Titus Titus, looking at me, grabbed a magician, sliced her throat, and left her body to fall. As he fled my advance, he caught magicians at random and killed them. It did not matter if they were on his side or not. By his action he was telling me to stop following him, and he was killing a token few to illustrate how many more he was willing and able to destroy. His ship rose from the valley and hovered above the battle. It sent a beam of light down to him but he still managed to grab one more magician from a duel and slice his head clean off his body.

He escaped into his ship and flew away across the sky, then up into the clouds and space beyond.

I could go after him. I could outfly his ship, but all around me lives were being lost for nothing. I'd had enough.

I had seen Adesua do it. I split myself into two, and each of the two into two more, and on and on, and each of me joined a fight. I experienced each of my selves and each of the battles that I took over, and there was no compromise to attention or ability. I was me, a thousand times in a thousand places, fighting a thousand battles, and yet I was the same person in all those places at the same time, facing a thousand different opponents and making a thousand different decisions at the same time. I was not divided. I was multiplied. I was in many places at the same time.

Each of the others had to fight me and the person they had been fighting before me. They had no chance. They saw me everywhere and realised what had happened. They saw their members falling dead from the sky. One by one they dropped their weapons. Some of them flew away while others stayed and offered their necks. I did not allow any surrendering magician to be killed.

When all of the others had either fled or stayed to join us, I brought myself back into one body. One by one the magicians descended to the ground, where the remains of our fallen friends and foes lay on soil red and wet with the blood that had rained down from the war above. To see the ground littered like that, with the limbs and torsos and gutted bodies of magnificent men and women who could take to the sky and fly, broke my soul. I managed a few steps through the carnage then I fell to my knees, buried my hands in my palms, and wept.

Chapter 60

E Pluribus Unum

I cried into my palms. My tears fell through my fingers onto the ground below. The blood-soaked soil gave up what it had drunk. The blood of the fallen seeped up through the ground, gathered around me and crawled up my body. Their blood covered me up to the crown of my head and dripped back to the ground below. Their voices wailed in agony, filling my soul.

I looked up. The magicians were standing around me.

'God help us,' someone said. 'He is going to kill us all.'

Everyone looked up to the sky where the magician pointed.

As I stood up, the blood washed off me and sank back into the ground. I followed the other magicians' gaze and I saw it too. It was nothing like I had ever seen before. It was a colour I had never seen before. It was a shape I had never seen before. It was as big as an entire city block and it must have been as heavy too, yet it sailed gently in the air towards us, the clouds parting in front of it long before it even reached them. On top of it, Titus Titus stood like an ant on the back of a whale.

The thing was a ship, but it was not from the Earth or the moon, and the beings inside it must have been the size of several dinosaurs.

I realised what Titus Titus had done. He had gone to another dimension only he could access, and he had brought back its inhabitants against whom our weapons were ineffectual and for whom our magic was non-existent. If he couldn't conquer the Earth, he meant to destroy it.

My mother made her way to the front of the crowd and stood between Adesua and Professor Ochuko.

'It has no shadow,' I said.

She looked under the thing at the valley it crossed, where its shadow should have been. 'What does that mean?' she asked.

'I know where it's from,' I said.

At that moment I understood that, during my time in the wilderness of the moon, and as I lay dying alone in a crater that would be my grave, it had not been an hallucination when Titus Titus took me away and showed me all the wonders I could roam and master, if only I would be like him and join the others. When he took me to all those places he hoped I would forsake my side of the divide for, we also came upon a place where shadows did not exist. It was to this place that he had gone to bring this entity that we were powerless against. All I had to do was find its antithesis which must exist in one of the countless universes that a magician such as Titus Titus could fly his ship to.

I stepped into a passage that was on my left. To the magicians watching me it would have appeared as if I had stepped halfway into an invisible door. They would have seen half of me still standing and the other half vanished. And then they would have seen the rest of me flatten like a board and fold back lengthwise, and the outer part of the fold would have vanished as well, leaving a slice of me that was flat, and only as wide as the measurement from the tip of my nose to the edge of my eye. And finally this slice of me that remained unsupported in the air would have folded in half and the two halves coming together would have vanished.

I had entered into not one, but several passageways all at once, as I had only seconds to find the thing that could defeat the shadowless beast before it got to the magicians. I had countless places to go in only a few seconds.

In one dimension I found a world where shadows were the past and the future, depending on the time of day, but this was not the thing I sought. In another place I found a world where it was the shadows that cast the beings, and not the other way round, but it too was not what I was looking for.

I searched a million places and discovered a trillion new things, but I did not stop until I found the one thing that could win the war for me, and the magicians, and all the lifeforms on Earth. When I found it I took it back with me. I led it down from the sky behind Titus Titus atop his shadowless being. Had he been able to, from where he stood atop his alien, he could have looked down and seen a shadow the size of a city, crawling over the hills and into the valley, gaining on his beast whose colour could not be described.

When an unstoppable force meets an immovable object, they slide together into a place where their meeting is possible; where the one cannot exist without the other. When a shadowless thing is matched with a thing-less shadow, together they become of the world where a shadow belongs to a thing and a thing has a shadow. They become of our world.

The shadow without a thing and the thing without a shadow aligned, and in an instant they became one thing and its shadow. And in that same instance gravity found the new thing, because on Earth, a mass the size of a city could not sail through the air.

It dropped from the sky and crashed into the valley below. The ground trembled with the force of several earthquakes, and a plume of dust several miles wide rose from the valley.

A blurred figure flew out of the cloud of dust. It was as Titus Titus.

I decided to show him what I could do.

I walked towards him where he hovered in the sky. Each step I took made me bigger by two, and as I grew, my human body transformed and I became the black void of the universe, and in me were all the galaxies and all their stars and all the planets and all the comets and everything else in all creation.

I stopped growing when my face was level with where

he stood in the sky. My head was the size of his entire body.

'You cannot do anything to me,' he said. 'I know who you are. I will say the word and you will let me go.'

'Go,' I said.

Only he heard it.

A hole opened up behind him. Its edges were like flowing water, entwining and morphing, and its centre was deep and black with the darkness of a place beyond planets and stars.

He cast his face to the right, to the fading glow and the orange rays that fanned out and coloured the still clouds, and his nose twitched.

'I never like this place. It's the smell of your sun. I can't stand it,' he said. 'It makes me want to kill and destroy.'

He looked at me. He floated backwards into the hole, to a place far from anywhere he thought I might already be waiting for him. The hole collapsed onto itself and vanished, and he was gone.

I turned and walked back to the magicians, reducing by half with each step until I was my normal size once more, and had changed back into my human form.

Professor Ochuko walked up to me and stood in front of me. He squinted as he looked into my eyes. He seemed to be searching for something. Then his face brightened with shock and with recognition and he said, 'E pluribus unum.'

The other magicians also looked at me as though they

had discovered something profound. They were silent and their hearts were filled with awe. They made way for me as I walked through the gathering to my mother and Adesua who stood side by side holding hands. They also looked at me with uncertainty and fear. I embraced them.

Chapter 61

Splitting Atoms

The sun set.

We formed a circle around the slain and held hands. I was happy to see Brother Moses on the other side of the circle from me. He was holding my mum's hand. My mum was holding Adesua's hand – I had left the two women to go and talk with Professor Ochuko who wanted to know where I'd been and what I'd seen there. Brother Moses smiled at me and winked, and I nodded in response.

Professor Ochuko raised his hands and, along with them, my hand and the hand of the magician on his other side. In two waves that swelled out from us, all the other magicians raised their hands as well.

Professor Ochuko began to hum a slow and mournful melody that all the other magicians knew. Sparks of fire danced across the bodies in the circle. The tiny sparks multiplied and formed a brilliant waving blanket of light that covered the departed.

The blanket of light rose slowly as we continued to hum and the bodies, now whole again, lifted off the ground with the light, and were carried up past our faces and up above our heads, and they continued rising as one solid body of beautiful, densely packed, brilliant white lights.

They rose up into the sky and kept rising, on and on, past the Earth's atmosphere, becoming a sparkling dot amidst the stars as they sailed on into space where great magicians are buried.

We all returned to the glasshouse. Not one person was injured, because magicians are efficient in war and always manage to kill.

Reginald the cat was holding court in the middle of a group of magicians that were laughing at his stories. For the first time I could hear what he was saying. He looked at me. He had felt me hearing him. He winked. I smiled and winked back. Brother Moses and my mother were listening to an old lady who I hadn't met.

Adesua was standing alone. She saw me looking at her. She turned and walked out into the night and I walked after her.

The full moon was radiant in the night sky. I spent a few moments gazing at it.

'We took Rachel home,' Adesua said. 'I know,' I said.

'She didn't want to go,' she said. 'I know.'

She stared at my face. She still showed no emotion. 'I'm not afraid of you, you know,' she said.

'I know.'

'Stop doing that. I don't want you to know. I just want you to be you.'

'Ok.'

She studied my face.

'He will return,' she said.

'I believe so.'

'What now?'

'How do you mean?'

'What will you do?'

'I lost something that belongs to you.'

'If you go, you might not return.'

'I know.'

'I don't want you to go.'

'Why?'

'Does it matter why? Would it make you stay?'

'No.'

'Then I will not tell you.'

'I understand.'

'So, what now?'

'I will go and get your soul back, and when I return we will continue to perform wherever we find an audience.'

'Just like that? Just like that.'

We both stood still and silent for a while. She looked over the valley upon which the other worldly thing lay destroyed and covered in shadows, like the humps of a mountain that had always been there.

She had asked me not to, so I did not know what was on her mind.

'Adesua,' I said, 'don't you find it strange that the day after the syzygy, the rest of the world went back to life as normal?'

'They were told it was a solar flare.'

'How did my mother know we were in trouble in Faka

fiki? She just happened to fly over?'

'Brother Moses called her.'

'When?'

'When Titus Titus held his leg. He had his phone on the other side. And he just happened to have his phone?'

'What are you getting at, Osaretin?'

I wasn't sure myself. It was a nagging feeling that I was still missing something. Something I'd not yet learned about myself, about magic, about Titus Titus. That there was more to everything that had happened than I yet fully understood, but when she said my name I smiled. She looked puzzled. 'What?' she said.

'That's the first time I've heard you say my name,' I said.

She looked away as if she didn't want me to see her smiling. She dug her hand into her pocket and took out a coin. She held it up. 'Remember this?' she said.

I nodded. It was Brother Moses' coin. The smile was still upon her face. It reminded me of when we first met.

She tossed the coin and hid it in her palm against the back of her hand.

'Heads,' I said.

She checked and she smiled even wider. She tossed the coin again.

'Heads.'

She checked and chuckled. We were like two kids playing our favourite game.

She tossed it again. While the coin was still spinning

350

in the air I called it, 'Heads.'

She caught the coin and checked it. Her smile wavered. It thinned out into a parted-lip uncertainty.

Before she picked the coin up again I called it. 'Heads.'

Her fingers shook as she picked up the coin and tossed it. It landed heads on the back of her hand.

She looked at me with eyes that were both in awe and terrified.

At that moment I saw her with a clarity with which I'd never seen her nor anyone before. It was a clarity that began in me, filled me up, and radiated from me, illuminating everything around. Her brown eyes yielded to me and let me see through to her mind and into her being. I travelled through every molecule that she was made of.

I saw her beginning and her end, and her every beginning and her every end. I saw all that she was and all that she could be. I saw her secrets, her fears, her hopes, her wishes, her past lovers, and her future lovers as well. I knew all of her weakness and all of her strengths. She could split atoms with her mind but she didn't know it. She once sat next to a master of the universe but she didn't notice. She would be cured of cancer before she was even diagnosed with it. She would continue to love me, then one day she would begin to resent me. The taste of vanilla ice cream would be the last thought on her mind as she died several decades away. I knew her from before she was born. From before her parents were born. From before she was formed in the womb.

I looked past her to the magicians in the glass house. Their secrets were open to me as if they had always been open to me. I looked around. Everything and every being revealed their pasts and their futures to me. I entered her mind and looked at myself through her eyes and saw what I was and what I had become. I wasn't myself any longer. I was the son, and I was my father, and I was something else as well – something that could go away and defeat death and bring back her soul even before I left.

Something that could call things that were not into being. Something that created universes and everything in them. Something powerful and awesome. Something magnificent and lonely.

I remembered everything. From the beginning and from every beginning I had created.

I once walked amongst humans. I wanted to know what they had become. And for a short while I forgot who I was, but that was also part of my plan.

The End